John Roy Musick

Saint Augustine

A Story of the Huguenots in America

John Roy Musick

Saint Augustine
A Story of the Huguenots in America

ISBN/EAN: 9783743400085

Manufactured in Europe, USA, Canada, Australia, Japa

Cover: Foto ©Raphael Reischuk / pixelio.de

Manufactured and distributed by brebook publishing software (www.brebook.com)

John Roy Musick

Saint Augustine

SAINT AUGUSTINE

A STORY OF THE HUGUENOTS IN AMERICA

BY

JOHN R. MUSICK

Author of "Columbia," "Estevan," "Pocahontas," Etc., Etc.

Illustrations by

FREELAND A. CARTER.

New York
FUNK & WAGNALLS COMPANY
London and Toronto
1895

PREFACE.

St. Augustine was founded during a period
which most historians seek to avoid. Mr. Bancroft
devotes but ten pages to it in his history of the
United States, and other historians have given it
even less space. A period so stained with blood
and crime is usually passed by as rapidly as possible by the historian, who doubtless shudders even
in his hurried march over the unpleasant ground.
And yet this period is one of the most important of
all the ages through which our country has passed.
At this time the Spaniards, a Catholic nation,
controlled the New World. The papal bull granted
to Spain all the countries discovered by Columbus,
and no Catholic nation dared violate that proclamation. The Pope declared that all the undiscov-
ered countries were God's, and he, as the representative of God, alone had power to bestow them on
the kings of the earth. But for the Reformation,

this country, in all probability, would have been a Spanish dominion or republic.

The story opens just when the great struggle for political and religious liberties was at its height. The author has endeavored to narrate impartially the events, without screening either Spanish, Catholic, or French Huguenot. Francisco Estevan, a native of Cuba, was a son of Christopher Estevan who served under Pizarro and De Soto, and a grandson of Hernando Estevan who came with Columbus on his first voyage. Francisco, by nature a soldier, was designed by his parents for the cloister, and as soon as he arrived at the age of maturity was sent to Spain to become a priest. Here, by accident, he met a beautiful Huguenot, Hortense De Barre, with whom he fell in love. His subsequent struggles with his conscience, his many adventures in the West Indies and in Florida, covering a period from 1560 to 1585, form the theme of this volume.

JOHN R. MUSICK.

Kirksville, Mo., March 1st, 1892.

TABLE OF CONTENTS.

LIST OF ILLUSTRATIONS.

vii

SAINT AUGUSTINE.

CHAPTER I.

THE DEPARTURE.

EARLY in Spanish American history, Havana, Cuba, became a
flourishing commercial city,
eclipsing all competitors, until
she reached what she is to-day,
the metropolis of the West
Indies. As early as 1561,
before any permanent set-
tlement had been made
within the present terri-
tory of the United States,
Havana was doing a flour-
ishing trade, and her magnificent harbor was
crowded with ships from Europe. The magnitude
of America was still unknown. As yet the Spaniards
were the only people who had crossed the ocean to
plant colonies on the western hemisphere. The West

1

Indies had been subjugated, Darien was under the dominion of Spain, and Mexico and Peru, those wonderfully civilized empires, were subjugated by the Spaniards with a sacrifice of life and cruelties shocking to the modern historian. Other nations of Europe were becoming aroused to the importance of American discoveries. Magellan's expedition around the world had established the proof that the earth was globular, a fact disputed by learned men about half a century before. The Cabots, sailing in the interest of England, and seeking for that chimerical northwest passage, which even modern navigators believe to exist, explored the Atlantic coast and Labrador. Verazzani, Cartier, and others, sailing under the French flag, had made some discoveries and taken possession of what is now Canada in the name of New France; but, as yet, there had been only discoveries. No permanent settlement had been formed except by the Spaniards.

All Europe, at this moment, was quaking with internal strife, which had much to do with deterring others from taking part in the conquests of America. The world was just on the eve of a revolution in religious thought. At the opening of our story Europe was just entering on the most important period of the world's history since the advent of the Saviour, the great Reformation.

Religious discussions as yet had not disturbed the New World. The Spaniards were a people of one faith. To them, the Roman Catholic Church was the door to heaven, guarded by St. Peter, and the only entrance for the soul into that eternal rest. To rebel against the church established by the Apostle Peter, from whom the Pope, in regular succession, received his authority, was, to the Spaniard, equivalent to a rebellion against God. Disputed questions were in those days settled by argument or the sword, and more frequently by the latter than the former. With religious feelings aroused, the quarrel became personal, and the persecutions bitter, while the oft-repeated words of the Master, "Peace and good will toward men," seemed to be forgotten.

To the Cubans, the struggle in Europe was a holy war, and many a battle-scarred pioneer, who had fought under Cortez, Pizarro, and De Soto, wished himself in Europe to take part in the struggle. The groans from Piedemonte, Toulouse, and other persecuted districts were heard around the world, but awoke no feeling of sympathy in the breasts of the bigoted Catholics of the West Indies.

One of the best families in the metropolis of the New World at this time was a family named Estevan. They did not occupy a high official position, for they had been constantly on the frontier, conquering, exploring, and colonizing, instead of courting the preference of kings and princes. The head of the family, Christopher Estevan, a namesake of Christopher Columbus, was the first child born of white parents in the New World. From infancy he had been associated with men whose names are familiar in history as conquerors. When a child, he sat on the knee of Cortez and Don Diego Columbus, who succeeded his father as admiral. He was with Pizarro in Peru, and attended the funeral of De Soto. His father, Hernando Estevan, had come with Columbus on his first voyage to America, and had always been a warm bosom friend of the great discoverer.

Christopher Estevan had removed to Havana from St. Jago several years before the date of our narrative, 1561. He was not old in years, being only fifty-two, but long exposure and numerous wounds received in battle prematurely aged the veteran.

A fortune amassed by his father in Mexico enabled him to live at ease with his beautiful wife, Señora Inez, one of the rarest flowers plucked from that land of beauty, old Spain. His home was a model of peace and happiness. Two sons and one daughter blessed his household, and he had retired from the field of battle and adventure covered with glory, and settled down to the enjoyment of a long, peaceful afternoon of life. Being a pious Catholic, he took more pleasure in religious services than in those wild scenes of daring which had delighted his youth. His greatest wish was to see his eldest son become a priest. Estevan knew of the allurements to conquest so abundant in this New World; but he believed that if his son were once in the cloister he would be safe from the ambitions and dangerous enterprises of the romantic age. Perhaps because Señor Estevan had disappointed his mother, who designed him for the church, he was the more determined that his son should follow the holy calling.

The dark-eyed, robust Francisco had been taught from early childhood to look upon himself as dedicated to the service of God. Educational facilities in the New World were not of the best, yet some pious monks had established an academy at which a number of young men were instructed in the sciences, theology and philosophy. Francisco was an apt scholar. His mind was clear, strong, and vigorous; but, though he was consecrated to the church, he seemed ill-fitted for the sacred calling. His flashes of wit, his love of athletic sports, his daring courage and fondness for romantic adventures made him more soldier than priest. Francisco, however, was loyal to the wishes of his parents, though he sighed when he remembered that the

wonders of those far-off lands, rumors of which
came in dreamy whispers to his ears, were never
to be explored by him.   His heart bounded in wild
delight when he heard his father tell of heroic
struggles with men and beasts in strange lands.
The pious youth checked all these natural impulses,
and lived a life of consecration.   His tutors were
highly elated at his progress, and assured the anxious parents that their son would be prepared soon
to don the sacerdotal robes.

Rodrigo, Francisco's brother, was nearly five
years younger than the intended ecclesiastic.   He
resembled his brother in form and feature, and
possessed to an eminent degree the same daring,
chivalrous spirit.   He loved the lance and the
saddle more than study, and his tutor was the cavalier rather than the priest.   Before he had reached
his sixteenth year, he had participated in several
expeditions by land and sea, and already had become conspicuous for his courage, prowess, and skill
in horsemanship.   Old cavaliers pronounced him
the best swordsman in Cuba, and in friendly combat he had disarmed many a veteran.

Francisco was to set out for Spain to complete
his ecclesiastical education under the old masters,
and Rodrigo, though only sixteen, had determined
to set forth in search of conquest and gold.   His
grandfather had participated in the conquest of

Mexico, winning a fortune there, consequently the youngest scion of this proud old Spanish family had chosen Mexico as the field for his operations. In those days Mexico and Peru were the great Eldorados, concerning which the wildest rumors of fabulous wealth were afloat. The credulous Cubans believed all they heard, however extravagant. Beyond the borders of the conquered territory there hung a veil of mystery which only the wildest conjecture could penetrate. Imagination, for the time being, supplanted reason and peopled those unknown regions with strange beings and marvellous riches excelling in wonder the mythology of the ancients. Rodrigo longed to plunge into the unknown realms, and drag into the light of civilization the hidden wonders of this mysterious world, and all efforts to dissuade him from this mad purpose were unavailing.

"Let brother Francisco become a friar if such is his wish, but I will be a soldier," declared Rodrigo.

The day came for the departure of the sons, one to Spain and one to Mexico. Two vessels which were to bear them away from their native island lay anchored in the harbor, side by side. Morning dawned bright and clear, and all nature was smiling with gladness. Havana at an early hour presented a scene of bustle and confusion. The harbor was melodious with the songs of sailors, while from the tropical forest, forming a semicircle about the town, came the sweetest music of those famous feathered warblers of the south.

In the home of Estevan there was more of sorrow than joy. Two beloved sons were about to depart for distant lands, and, in those troublous times, parents knew that many went and few returned. It would perhaps be the last time they would gaze on the faces of their children. Francisco and Rodrigo were on the balcony of the house when the sun rose.

"Rodrigo," said Francisco, seizing his brother's hand, "Many times have we stood thus and watched the sun rise. Does it occur to you this morning that we may never witness this glorious scene together again?"

"In truth, good brother, I had not thought about it at all."

"Where were your thoughts?"

"In the unknown regions I am to explore, Francisco. Pardon me if I am not as sober and sedate as my brother; I have no thoughts save for conquest."

"Yet, on this eventful morning, when we are to separate, perhaps never to meet again, might it not be well for the cavalier to give himself up to sober thought?"

"Where would be the use, my brother? It would only make the heart ache. The ills which

we are to suffer will come full soon without brood-
ing over prospective calamities; and when the day
comes, if come it must, let us meet it bravely, I
with the resolution of a soldier and you with the
resignation of a priest."

"I must admit you are a philosopher as well as
a soldier."

"Nay, do not credit me with qualities I do not
possess. Call me a soldier with all a soldier's
qualifications—nothing more."

"Philosophy is essential even to men of arms."

"Then, so far as essential, let me be a philosopher; but I must confess, my brother, that the
prospect of a brilliant career in Mexico robs our
parting of its bitterness. I love my parents,
brother, and sister, and I would belie my feelings
were I to say I experience no regret, yet the
thought of entering on a brilliant career to a great
extent overbalances this sentiment."

Francisco gazed on the youthful face of his
brother, lighted with a glow of enthusiasm, and
heaved a sigh. Rodrigo, young as he was, had
reached a man's stature, and his gallant figure
made him an object of admiration. Francisco
never saw him in the tourney on his fiery charger,
caparisoned in glittering steel, that he did not wish
to be like him.

"Brother," he said at last, breaking a silence

that was growing painful, "let us make a compact,
which, if we live, shall be carried into effect."

"What shall it be?" asked Rodrigo.

"When we meet again, let it be to part no more.
We may be aged and infirm, you bowed down with

hardship and wounds, and
in need of a brother's care."

The youthful face of
Rodrigo grew thoughtful
for a moment.

"It shall be as you say,
brother," he said, "and as
our childhood was passed
together, so shall be our
old age. I regret even
this short separation, and
wish I could go with you,
not as a priest, but as a soldier in the holy war against
the Protestants, who are
striving to overturn the

RODRIGO ESTEVAN.   power of the Pope."

A cloud came over Francisco's brow, and for a
moment his dark eye flashed with religious zeal.

"Deluded people, led by such unholy men as
Luther and Melancthon," he murmured, "but the
Inquisition has been re-established and will root
out the heretics from Spain. The war will be car-

ried even into France, England, and Germany, if need be, until the Roman Catholic faith is again supreme in the world. The trust confided by Saint Peter by regular succession to our holy father will not be wrested from him."

"I am willing to draw my sword against the Protestant as did our ancestors against Saracens."

"That day may come. Yet Protestants are mingled with Catholics as tares grow in the wheat, and the winnowing will require care. Heresy is sown by the devil while we sleep. It takes root in some families, and ere we know it a son, a daughter, a brother, or a sister, has become imbued with these dangerous ideas, and we must then give them over to their fate. Yet I do not believe it right to burn them at the stake, or to slay them, as is done in Spain, France, and England."

"What would you do? The tares must be uprooted."

"No, that would destroy the wheat. Let all grow together until the harvest, when the Master shall winnow the wheat and cast the tares in the fire to be burned."

An end was put to the discussion by the father calling to them to come down. Owing to an old wound, Señor Estevan was compelled to walk with a staff. The mother and the young sister, a beautiful child of the tropics, with the father were at

the breakfast table, awaiting the young men. The
morning meal was eaten in silence; then the young
men were embraced by their parents, and the
mother, with moist eyes and faltering voice, proceeded to give her parting injunctions to them.

"Rodrigo, you go to a life of conquest and danger. Be not rash or cruel. Ever let mercy and
caution prompt you, and amid scenes of greatest
danger remember your mother. Think how lonely
she will be here without a son as the prop and stay
of her declining years. When you have satiated
your ambition for conquest as your father did, return to live a life of ease and quiet, the joy and
comfort of your parents for the remainder of their
lives." Turning to her eldest son, she said: "O
Francisco, you are the delight and joy of your
mother. Be loyal to the church, and when you
have taken the monastic vows and donned the
sacerdotal robes of the priesthood, remember that
your mother willingly gave you to the service of
God. Be a loyal priest, and seek to serve your
Master by penance and prayer. Let your future
be devoted to your sacred calling. Bind up the
broken heart, carry the Gospel into the wilderness
among the heathen, and thus aid in bringing all
the world to the true religion."

The father's parting injunctions to his sons were
similar to the mother's. He urged on his younger

a course of manliness as well as courage, advised
him never to be wantonly cruel or foolishly brave,
and pointed out Pizarro as an example of a petty
tyrant. The bravest were usually most gentle and
kind.

Then came the sister, only a child in years, too
young to give advice. She brought them only a
small token—two locks of golden hair clipped from
her own fair head, to be worn near their hearts
as mementos of one who loved them. The little
girl was named Christoval after a dear foster-sister
of her father. She was unlike her brothers, quite
fair, with blue eyes, which on this occasion were
overflowing with tears. She was too young to
entirely control herself at the parting, and though
no sobs escaped her lips, those silent tears, trickling
down her pretty cheeks, were stronger evidences
of real grief than sobs or groans.

The vessels were to sail at an early hour, and the
little party wended their way to the beach. Rodrigo's horse, arms, armor, and baggage had already
been taken aboard the vessel, and Francisco had
made similar preparations. He walked to the
beach between his mother and sister, holding a
hand of each, but, though he assumed a cheerful
manner, his heart was very heavy. A whirlwind
of thought swept through his mind at this moment.
His desire to be a soldier and overturn kingdoms

as his father had done and brother was to do, was
strong; but to reap the golden harvest of conquest
was denied him; long before he had arrived at the
age of accountability, his course in life had been
marked out.

At the beach the brothers embraced parents and
sister; then, embracing each other, they entered
separate boats, and were rowed to their respective
ships. Sitting in the stern of his boat, Francisco,
through his tear-dimmed eyes, alternately glanced
at the little group on shore and the other boat
bearing away his brother. His manhood was
shaken to its centre, and he could scarce restrain a
flood of tears. He reached the ship bound for
Spain and went aboard. There came the usual
noise of hoisting anchor and getting under way.
The creaking of cordage, the cries of officers, and
the confused noises which may be heard on any
sailing vessel floated over the harbor to the little
party on shore.

During the entire preparation, Francisco stood
on the deck gazing one moment at the shore and
next at his brother's ship. Both anchors were
hoisted at nearly the same time, and, as Francisco
waved his cap at the ship of his brother, the stunning reports of two lombards shook the sea and
told that the vessels were under way. A moment
later the shores echoed and re-echoed with the

salute fired from the castle and fort. The breeze
was strong and the ships bore away rapidly, leav-

THE REPORT OF TWO
LOMBARDS SHOOK
THE SEA.

ing the native island
farther and farther in the distance, until
Cuba was but a dim speck in the horizon. Then Francisco turned his gaze
to the vessel which was bearing his
brother away. Farther and farther the

ships drifted apart, until Francisco could only see a snowy speck on the horizon, which at last disappeared altogether. Long after the sail had faded from view, the student stood gazing in the direction of it.

"My brother goes to war and I to peace."

Had he been able to read the future, he would have seen that no peace or cloister was in store for him, but a wild whirlpool of excitement. No sacerdotal robe was ever to grace his form. In the name of religion he was to witness such scenes of blood and crime as almost to disgust him with the holy order, and he was to be more of a soldier than a priest. But let us await the fulness of time and not anticipate events.

CHAPTER II.

THE world had reached that age of earnest theological discussion and antagonism in Europe, known as the "Era of the Reformation." Martin Luther and Philip Melancthon, in Germany, led a revolt against the Italian hierarchy, as rulers in the Christian Church, whose head was the Pope of Rome. A similar revolt, headed by Zuingliss, had broken out in Switzerland, and the Pope trembled lest his universal power should be swept away from him. Historians designate the time as a moment of intellectual liberty—the perfect equality of all men in Church and State, in the exercise of the inalienable rights of private judgment in matters of politics and religion. It was at the Diet or Congress held at Spires in 1529 that Luther and several princes in sympathy with him entered their solemn *protest*, which to this day has characterized their followers of all denominations and creeds as *Protestants*. They found the mother church so strong, that they were compelled to form a league

2   17

against it, and so first organized the Reformation as an aggressive moral power leading to theological and political combinations, · which, twenty-five years later, freed the Germans from the domination of the Italian church.

But the Romish church was not disposed to yield its supremacy in the Christian world without a desperate struggle, and it put forth all its energies for the maintenance of its power. It had mighty agencies in its traditions, its vantage-ground of possession, the Order of Jesuits which it had just created, and the Inquisition which it had re-established with new powers. Its warfare was keen and terrible, and its victories were many; but, despite all that power and persecution could do, the Reformation gained ground in certain parts of Europe. In the heat of that conflict was evolved the representative government, the free institutions, and the liberty, equality, and fraternity which are the birthright of every American citizen to-day without regard to creed.

In no part of the civilized world did the Reformation meet with more determined enemies in court and church than in France. John Calvin, the chief reformer in that country, was banished, and, taking refuge in Switzerland, died in the year 1564. But Calvin had sowed the seeds of Protestantism in France, and those seeds bore fruit in such daring

persons as Admiral Coligni, the favorite of Catharine de Medici while she was acting as regent for
her son the infant king. Thus the most conspicuous leader of the Huguenots, as the French Protestants were called, found means of reaching the
royal ear. All parties admired Coligni for his
gallant services to his country. He persuaded
Catharine to attempt to reconcile by a conference
the contending religious factions; but the peace
conference failed and war ensued. The Duke of
Guise, a lineal descendant of Charlemagne, and
claimant of the French throne, a man whom Catharine both feared and hated, led the Roman Catholics, while the Prince of Conde headed the Protestants. The latter, being much in the minority,
suffered greatly in the contest. Perhaps never,
even in savage warfare, was cruelty carried further
than in this conflict between religious factions.

At this time there lived in Dieppe a prominent
and once wealthy sea-captain named De Barre.
For important services rendered the king certain
rights and privileges were granted him. He was
a lover of civil and religious liberties, and when
the Reformation began to shake the world with its
thunder, De Barre, a cousin of Coligni, under whom
he had served in the royal navy, espoused the cause
of Protestantism. The sea-captain's family con-
sisted of himself, wife, and two children, a son

aged eighteen and, like his father, a sailor, and a daughter Hortense who had just reached her fifteenth year. Hortense De Barre, though still a child, showed such promises of beautiful womanhood that she had admirers even among the nobility. One of her most ardent suitors was a young Frenchman of means but of doubtful morals, named John Gyrot.

Gyrot was troubled with no serious religious convictions. His views were flexible and could be adjusted to suit either Huguenot or Papist. He early evinced an admiration, which grew into a consuming passion, for the beautiful Hortense; but when he one day mentioned the matter to her, the child, who had never yet entertained a thought of marriage, fled in terror from the bold, ardent young man. Gyrot possessed determination to a remarkable degree, in fact it was about his only virtue, and he resolved to possess this lily of France, whose large blue eyes and golden hair had enslaved him.

In one of those terrible religious riots the home of the De Barres was destroyed, the father and son were killed, and the mother died from fright and grief the same day. Thus like an avalanche came down upon the innocent young head all the thunderbolts of hate and fanaticism. Hortense, left alone in the world with no relative save her father's cousin,

who was in Paris at the time, took temporary refuge among some kind people who agreed to shelter
her for a while, and as soon as practicable send her
out of the country, for the bold utterances of the
father had so incensed the Catholics that his innocent child was threatened with the stake.

While still at the house of her friends, her
cousin, Coligni, hearing of her great bereavement
and wretched condition, came to see her. Poor
Hortense, quite heart-broken, was overcome at sight
of her only relative on earth and fell sobbing in
his arms. As he held the child close to his own
kind heart, and tried to soothe her grief and fears,
the good man gazed into the pure innocent face
pityingly.

"All this is done in the service of God?" he
murmured. "Rather say in the service of the
devil, for God abhors such misery." Appealing
once more to the child he said, "Cheer up, sweet
cousin, you shall suffer no further harm."

"Yes, yes! they will put me to death, they will
burn me at the stake for heresy."

"They shall not," he answered.

"What is heresy?" she asked innocently.

"So they would destroy one so young and innocent that she does not understand the meaning of
the offence of which she is charged. This is infa-
mous." Addressing the child he answered, "Never

mind now, little one, you will know the definition
of the word when you are older. I will send you
for the present to Beaucarre, a village on the Mediterranean, until we can transport all the persecuted
to that new world discovered by Verazzani and
Cartier."

Hortense dried her tears and tried to smile.

"I want to go to the new country where I shall
be free from persecution," she said.

"You shall, little cousin, you shall."

"When?"

"I must first see the king and obtain a grant
for a colony of the persecuted. All this will
take time; meanwhile you will be safe at Beaucarre."

"Can I go in the first ship?"

"No, you must wait until explorers and pioneers
are sent to select a location and build houses."

A look of disappointment came over the pretty
face and a sigh escaped her lips. Coligni noted
her anxiety to leave France.

"Don't despair, child," he added, "you shall
suffer no more persecution. At Beaucarre you
are in a quiet, out-of-the-way part of the world,
free from the great turmoil and strife which upsets
civilization to-day and make savages of men."

Addressing a few more words of consolation to
her, the great admiral, strangely impressed at her

sad fate, left the child. In the corridor, Coligni met a person not calculated to inspire the beholder with confidence. He was attired in dark velvet doublette, black trunk hose to his thigh, and long, dark stockings. He wore a sable cloak on his shoulders, a crimson cap on his head, and the sword at his side seemed to indicate that he made some pretensions to being a gentleman. Though a young man scarce twenty, his face, pale and cadaverous, had the appearance of age. A quantity of black hair descended low over his eyebrows, while the small, black, piercing eyes and lines of the face denoted shrewdness. The glance of this individual was keen, but evinced cunning rather than intelligence. His lips were straight, but so thin that, as they closed, they were compressed within his mouth. His cheek-bones were broad and projecting, a never-failing proof of audacity and craftiness, while the flatness of his forehead and the enlargement of the back of the skull, which rose much higher than the vulgarly shaped ears, combined to form a physiognomy anything but prepossessing.

Coligni paused a moment and glanced at the young man as he sauntered toward him.

"That fellow has a bad countenance," he declared mentally. "Why is it that all do not retreat with aversion at sight of that flat, receding,

serpent-like forehead, round skull and sharp
hooked nose like the beak of a vulture?"

This personage seemed watching the admiral
with a shrewd, cunning gaze as though he mis-
trusted the object of his visit. Once the admiral
laid his hand on his sword as if to punish his inso-
lence; but, perceiving his youth, he concluded
that no harm could come from him. As Coligni
retired, a diabolical grin illuminated the face and
increased its ugliness. Had the admiral noted the
change he would have paused to inquire more
about the young man he had met in the corridor.

Scarcely was Coligni out of sight, when this personage entered the chamber of Hortense De Barre
without even the formality of knocking. The
girl's face became troubled at sight of him.

"Why do you come here, John Gyrot?" she
asked.

"I want to ask the mademoiselle some questions," Gyrot answered.

"Ask them, and be gone at once."

"Who was the stranger who has just left?"

"Coligni."

"The admiral?"

"Yes."

"I heard him say he was going to send the
mademoiselle to Beaucarre, and, as the mademoiselle has refused the hospitality I offered her, I,

too, will go to Beaucarre to keep guard over her in these trying times."

Hortense started and became deathly pale. There was something cunning and significant in Gyrot's manner, and she trembled, though unable to tell why. Gyrot had not, to her knowledge, taken any part in the outbreak against the Huguenots. On the contrary he pretended to be in sympathy with the Protestants; but there was something so hypocritical in these pretences that she lacked confidence in him. She wanted to tell him that his services were not needed; but she was so young and shy that she could make no answer, and hung her head in silence, while Gyrot in his disagreeable tone continued:

"I am quite a man now. The mademoiselle needs a protector, and where can she find a better one than Monsieur Gyrot?"

At this point she plucked up sufficient courage to assure him that her relative had made all needful arrangements for her safety and comfort; but he was persistent in his determination to be her guardian and protector, and she was glad when he went away. She had known Gyrot from early childhood, and, while he had ever pretended to be a devoted friend of the family, she instinctively felt an aversion for him.

Meanwhile, Coligni, whose great heart was

touched at the forlorn condition of the child, as well as the desperate situation of all the Huguenots, resolved to secure an asylum for them in the milder regions of North America, where, far removed from civilized men, they might enjoy that perfect religious and civil freedom for which they sighed.

Soon after the touching interview with his unfortunate little cousin, he sought an audience with Catharine de Medici, which was readily granted. That proud and unprincipled woman, then little more than forty years of age, stout and fair, was wielding with a prodigal hand the power she assumed through her infant son.

Coligni was not without his misgivings, for, while the king's mother was his friend, he knew she was selfish and fickle and liable at the last moment to refuse the dearest wish of his heart, a place of refuge for the persecuted.

He had consulted with John Ribault, an experienced mariner, who was willing to undertake the hazardous task of planting a French colony on the new-found coast, and he needed only a charter and means to send the Huguenots to America.

Coligni was tall, elegant in figure and deportment, grave in aspect, with flowing hair and beard slightly streaked with gray, for he was about forty-five years of age. On his visit to Catharine he was dressed in the uniform of his rank, wearing on his head a rich green velvet cap bearing an ostrich plume. His doublette of crimson velvet with skirt was sprinkled with golden lilies and encircled with a belt from which depended a straight sword. The sleeves terminated at the elbows; the remainder of his arms to the wrists were covered with embroidered linen. His trunk hose of velvet extended to the middle of his thighs, and was slashed and elegantly embroidered with gold thread. Up to this, tight fitting stockings wrought of fine white wool extended, and on his feet were buskins of polished russet leather, sparkling with diamond buttons that were fastened with silk rosettes to the insteps. From his shoulders hung an open, short Spanish cloak of blue velvet, and around his neck a modest ruff. A massive gold chain bearing the order of St. Louis was seen upon his breast. Such was the appearance of this great and good man as he asked an audience with the Regent of France, late in the year 1561, to confer with her upon the subject of discoveries and the planting of a colony in America.

He had not long to wait. The court dignitary to whom he applied soon returned with the information that the admiral could be admitted to the presence of her majesty at once. With his cap in his hand, perfectly self-possessed, he entered the royal

presence.   He was only to meet a woman and a boy,
a mere child.   The woman he knew was unprincipled, yet, for the present, she was friendly to
the Protestant cause, more because she hated the
Duke of Guise than from any serious religious
convictions.

Coligni found her seated on a rich divan covered
with blue damask satin.   On her head was a coronet, sparkling with a single large diamond.
Around her plump neck glittered a circlet of gold
and pearls, emeralds and rubies.   She wore a skirt
of gold-embroidered white silk, and over this a
rich robe of royal purple velvet, trimmed with a
narrow band of ermine at the front and bottom, and
with close-fitting bodice, linen and lace, with brilliant gems at the wrists.   A gold chain, fastened at
her bosom with a diamond brooch, extended to her
feet and terminated with a golden cross studded
with seed pearls.   Near her, playing with a fawn-
colored Italian greyhound, was her royal son, who
had lately been crowned as CHARLES IX., king of
France.   The young king's hair hung in ringlets
about his shoulders, for he was only a boy ten or
twelve years of age, thinking more of his dog than
of his kingdom.   His fair complexion was height-
ened by his rich suit of royal purple velvet, with
slashed sleeves, revealing white linen beneath.
Only a single minister of state was present, and he

and a young woman, a court favorite and cousin of the king of Navarre, were the only companions of royalty when Admiral Coligni entered the room.

The admiral bowed his knee and kissed the hand which Catharine gave him, performing a like ceremony to his sovereign who fondled his dog.

"Rise, admiral, and state your business," said the regent.

Coligni proceeded in a grave, earnest manner to inform her of the persecution of the Huguenots. She listened, though evincing no emotion at the the terrible recital, while the king, wholly engrossed with his greyhound, heard but little that the admiral said.

When Coligni began to particularize and related in detail the sad story of Hortense De Barre, the young lady left her seat in the window, and the minister of state, who had been urged to remain, listened with most rapt attention. The mob in all its terrible fury was depicted, the death of father, brother and mother related as only the eloquent Coligni, in the fervor of his enthusiasm, could tell it.

When he had finished, the king's mother asked:

"What do you propose, admiral, to alleviate the suffering of these poor people?"

"I am just approaching the plan, your majesty,

which will not only furnish an asylum for the persecuted Huguenots, but will redound to the honor and glory of France. In America, Verazzani, under the flag of France, made some wonderful discoveries, and took possession of the country under the name of *New France*. These, with the discoveries and conquests of Cartier, gave us valuable possessions in that land."

At this point the king's mother interposed:

KING CHARLES IX.

"But Cartier's report of his second voyage was by no means cheering. The rigors of the climate in winter, the ice-bound condition of the streams for several months in the year, and the utter barrenness of the land in precious stones and minerals were discouraging."

"Quite true, your gracious majesty; but subsequent voyages have proved that south of where Cartier explored there is a more favorable climate and soil. Donnacona, the Indian chief whom Cartier brought captive to France, told of the large number of fur-bearing animals in the woods and waters, of which Cartier could know nothing. These animals, with the salmon fisheries and pine forests, make even that apparently undesirable locality a valuable acquisition to France."

The princess regent nodded her head until the diamond in her coronet sparkled like a twinkling star, and the boy king, looking up from his dog, said:

"Give the admiral all the territory he wants; surely we have a plenty for all."

Next moment he fell to fondling his dog again and seemed to have forgotten the order he had issued to his mother. Nor was his command heeded. Catharine thought for her son, and seldom allowed the king, even in more mature years, the power of exercising his own will.

Coligni was a good judge of human nature. He read the king's mother like an open page, and for various reasons knew that she would ultimately consent to his plan; but he allowed no stone to go unturned, and proceeded with his argument which the king had interrupted.

"It is not in the cold north that I design to plant your colony, but the milder climate of that region known as Florida. Unexplored, possessing untold riches, and of a climate mild as Italy's, it is the land which France should claim, and it will redound to the glory of your son's reign if you acquire it."

"Do not the Spaniards, the original explorers, claim the land?"

"They have forfeited their right by abandoning it," the admiral answered. "Ponce de Leon, Hernando de Soto, and others who have invaded this land, so rich in natural resources, abandoned it, and since then. the whole coast has been seized in the name of the king of France, and it is ours."

The princess regent was not hard to persuade into compliance with his wishes. She granted all that Coligni desired, in the name of the little king, then playing with the greyhound, and the child's signature, hardly legible, was afterward placed to the charter given the admiral, by which he was authorized to send an expedition to Florida to establish a colony in the name of France.

Coligni lost no time in making use of his privilege. He hastened to Dieppe, where he found John Ribault and an English youth, Walter Raleigh, who was interested in the cause of the Huguenots, awaiting his return.

"Have you succeeded?" asked Ribault.

"I have the charter. Now, captain, proceed at once to organize your crews and colony. What you do is done in the name of God and humanity."

Ribault, like Coligni, was a zealous Huguenot, and was fired with enthusiasm at the thought of planting a colony in the New World. Coligni was the main support of the enterprise. It was not difficult to get colonists, for those who had suffered from persecution were only too anxious to find an asylum in the New World. Only men were taken in the first expedition, as it was a pioneer exploring party. Ribault was a native of Dieppe, and an experienced sailor, so that he inspired great confidence in the hearts of the people, who were eager to volunteer under so valiant a leader. Two vessels of the character of Spanish caravels were fitted out, and on the 18th. of February, 1562, Ribault sailed from Dieppe with two crews, consisting of excellent sailors, and a strong body of land forces, among whom were several gentlemen volunteers.

The first land discovered was low and woody, and he gave it the name of Cape Français. Turning to the right, he discovered the river Dauphin, without entering it; then sailed to the river May, so called from his entering it on the first day of that month. Here he was welcomed by a great number of the natives, and he erected a stone column on which the arms of France were engraved. This ceremony being performed, he visited the cacique of the savages and made him some presents. He afterward steered for the river Jourdain which had been discovered by Vasquez, and, keeping in sight of land, sailed along the coast of what is now known as the Carolinas. Arriving at the river of St. Croix, he built, in the midst of a most delightful country, Fort Charles, in honor of the king.

3

The neighboring rivers abounded in fish, the forest was filled with game, and the savages seemed so extremely friendly that the colonists thought they had entered the promised land. Having planted the germ of the future colony, Ribault returned to France, hoping soon to remove the women and children of the persecuted Huguenots to this place of refuge.

The foregoing may seem to be a digression; but if the reader will bear with us, it will be found to be an essential explanation to our story before it is finished.

Scarcely had John Ribault sailed from Dieppe, when Coligni took his cousin's child, Hortense De Barre, to the village of Beaucarre on the Mediterranean.

They arrived at the village, and she was installed with the family of Monsieur Beaumonte, half aubergiste and half fisherman. Beaucarre was never a thriving village, and to-day only a few ruins mark the spot where it once stood. Its very isolation made it an acceptable place of refuge for the persecuted girl.

It was late when she reached Beaucarre, and Hortense retired without inspecting her new home; but at early morn, childlike, she arose and set out to see what it was like. The house was a sort of an old inn of the time, standing beyond the hamlet, and from the front hung a sign. The place boasted a garden, consisting of a small plot of ground, a full view of which could be obtained from the door, immediately opposite the ground portal by which travellers were ushered in to partake of the hospitality of the public house. This *plaisance*, or garden, scorched beneath the ardent sun of an almost tropical latitude, permitted nothing to thrive and scarcely anything to live in its arid soil. A few dingy olives and stunted fig-trees struggled hard for existence, but their withered, dusty foliage proved how unequal was the conflict. Between these sickly shrubs grew a scant supply of garlic, tomatoes, and eschalots, while lone and solitary, like a forgotten sentinel still on duty, a tall pine reared its melancholy head in one of the corners of this unattractive spot.

At places in the surrounding plain, which more resembled a dusty lake than the solid ground, were scattered a few miserable stalks of wheat, the result of an effort on the part of the agriculturists of the country to see if it were possible to raise grain in this parched region. The scanty produce served to accommodate the numerous grasshoppers with resting-places upon the stunted specimens of horticulture, while they filled the air with sharp, unpleasant cries.

Poor Hortense gazed over the scene, unattractive

save where the waters of the Mediterranean broke on the shore, and sighed.

"Better if I had gone with the first emigrants to the New World," she thought.

At this moment she caught sight of a person on horseback riding over the dusty plain toward her. One glance at his face and she trembled and turned pale.

It was John Gyrot.

CHAPTER III.

Two years had elapsed since Estevan's arrival in Spain. He was progressing well with his studies and could already repeat the Latin prayers and church service. He was meek, humble, and very studious. The good Father Ronoldo had, from the first, taken great interest in his pupil and watched over him as a natural father might. Letters came from his parents at home and the brother in Mexico. Rodrigo's letters were filled with most marvelous descriptions of the wonderful land and people among whom his lot was cast. His accounts of some of his thrilling adventures made the heart of the intended ecclesiastic leap within him.

Though everything possible was done to make Francisco happy he grew paler and more sad day by day, until the good father Ronoldo became alarmed for his health. One day he entered the study of Francisco as the student was pouring over a volume of commentaries.

449813

"My son, you study too hard."

"Why do you say so, father?"

"Your cheek grows paler and your form thinner than I care to see it."

"A monk must needs be a student."

"Tell me, Francisco, are you happy?"

The unexpected question was asked in such an earnest manner that Francisco could not but feel the thought in the priest's mind.

"Why do you ask?" he gasped.

"Beause you do not seem it."

"Would you have me merry, father? Is not ours a sacred calling in which solemnity should become a part of us?"

"True, yet with solemnity and gravity there should be a quiet joy in the knowledge that we are servants of God. Answer me truly, do you really wish to become a priest?"

Françisco bounded to his feet as suddenly as if he had been pricked with the point of a sword, and faced the priest.

"Have I ever by word or deed indicated that such was not my desire?" he asked.

"No, my son; but you do not look as if you loved the holy order."

"I do—of course I do!" he answered quickly. "It is their choice. From my infancy I was designed for the church."

The priest gazed a moment at the agitated face, and shook his head knowingly.

"Parents may make a mistake," he remarked; "but I will not gainsay their wishes. Why should not a parent consecrate a child to God in this modern day as in ancient times? But methinks, my son, when they made you a priest, Spain lost a gallant soldier."

Estevan clasped his hand over his heart, and turned an appealing glance on the priest as if to implore him to desist. Interpreting his thought the ecclesiastic added:

"I have come to talk with you on other matters, my son—the heretics, for instance."

"Do they increase?"

"Verily, in places they do. That Luther is a bold fellow. Calvin was driven from France; but he had sown the bad seed before his departure, and the air is filled with heresy."

"Does not the Inquisition uproot it?"

"It does much, but not enough. The good Duke of Guise, the gallant defender of the faith, is battling for the Pope; but Coligni seems to hold control over the king's mother, regent to the infant king Charles, and, saints preserve us! I know not how it will end."

Here the priest paused and crossed himself. A moment later his features brightened,

"There is another matter I wanted to speak with you about," he said. "Some Benedictine monks are going to make a pilgrimage to the Pope. Would you like to go to Rome?"

"I would," Estevan answered, "Give me a journey and it will recuperate my failing spirits."

"Then you shall go."

It was arranged in a few days, and Estevan, in company with the pilgrims, set out for Rome. They travelled on mules to a little seaport town on the Mediterranean, and embarked in a vessel for Italy. Their vessel was a large Spanish caravel, a goodly craft, laden with wine. The captain was an experienced seaman and his crew one of the best. Spanish sailors had won a reputation for being among the boldest and most successful navigators of the day.

The weather was a little hazy, but there was nothing formidable in the appearance of the sky to a bold and experienced navigator. Francisco Estevan was something of a sailor, and, having been reared in the West Indies, was familiar with hurricanes. Scarcely had they been under way an hour when a gale sprang up which rapidly increased to a violent storm, separating them from the land at the rate of eight leagues a watch, merely with their fore-courses, insomuch that the master thought it necessary to stop that career, and, on consulting with his officers, brought the ship about and tried to furl up sails in order to make headway with the mizzen. The mountainous seas, the early product of the storm, became so unruly that the seamen knew not how to work the ship. They were already some distance from land, so that immediate danger from reefs and surfs was not great; but so violent was the storm, they were in danger of foundering, especially as the ship rocked in the hollow trough of the sea. With great exertion and danger, the main yard was lowered to give some case to the mast. Then the great difficulty was to handle the fore-sails, that the ship might work about with as little hazard as possible. All hands were not enough to haul the sheet close, in order to bring the ship about.

Francisco Estevan volunteered his services, and his former experience on shipboard made the young theologian quite useful. Great seas were shipped as the vessel came to work through the trough of the sea. One wave broke upon the poop where the monks were quartered, and a ton's weight of water set all afloat in the round-house. The noise made by the rushing wave was like the report of a great gun, and put the pilgrim monks into a sad fright. Many were on their knees, others were counting their beads, or offering prayers, or making promises of pilgrimages.

The shock being past, the vessel put about, with foresail hauled, and now lay trying with her mizzen to make headway. Tossed like a feather on the foam-capped waves, the water leaping in terrible fury over the deck, the ship, it seemed, could not hold together. Those awful sounds, heard only in a storm at sea, the roaring of the wind through the rigging like shrieks of demons, with the groans of the laboring ship, put the monks in deadly fear. Hours wore on and a dark and terrible night set in, the enraged seas a mass of seething foam, the gale still increasing, their condition growing more and more terrible every moment. A loud crash aloft, and the foremast came by the board, broken short off just under the cap. Francisco and his companions started to inquire the cause of the disaster, when a mighty sea broke on the foreship, making such an inundation on the deck which he had gained, that he retired to the round-house, a prayer on his lips, for he supposed the ship was foundering. The vessel stood stock-still, her head under water, as though to bore her way into the sea. The monks took a short leave of each other, and, assailed by new terrors, made a dolorous outcry, while the captain, seeing the deck almost cleared of water, called aloud:

"Man the pumps!"

Francisco, having better sea-legs than his companions, again ventured to look out, and learn the cause of this astonishing alarm, which appeared to arise from a no less cause than the loss of the forecastle, with five guns and the ship's anchors, all of which were fastened to the cable. Two men had been swept overboard and lost in the surging billow. The great gap made in the forecastle opened a passage into the hold for other seas; but luckily they had a number of ship's carpenters aboard, and these partially repaired the damages.

Throughout the long, terrible night the ship weathered the storm and at dawn of day was little more than a battered hulk. The day for which all had so earnestly prayed came at last, but brought no abatement in the storm. Those white, fleecy clouds held no promise for the future. The wind roared, the waves raged, and all day long the ship labored in the turbulent waters.

When the sun again went down the storm increased. The clouds grew thicker and blacker, and, charged with electricity, sent streams of liquid fire over the awful scene.

"The ship cannot live through the night," Francisco heard the captain declare.

The bowsprit, having lost its stays and rigging, and being too heavy in itself, swayed to and fro with such bangs that they were compelled to cut it off to prevent the whole front part of the ship

from being demolished. Everything was in a
miserable state of disorder, and it was evident
their danger was increasing every moment. The
stays of all the masts were gone, the shrouds that
remained were loose and useless, and it was easy to
foresee that the mainmast must soon come by the
board. A brave Portuguese sailor, always ready
to expose himself to danger for the welfare of
others, seized a carpenter's axe and ran up to prevent the evil, hoping to ease the mainmast and
preserve it; but the danger to his person was so
manifest that the captain called him down, and no
sooner had his foot touched the deck than with a
fearful crash both main and top-mast came down
together, falling to windward clear of the deck into
the sea without harming any one.

The shrouds and rigging retaining their hold on
the vessel's side, at every surge of the sea, like a
monster pattering ram, the butt of the broken mast
was driven against the side of the vessel, threatening to beat a hole through it. The Portuguese now
with his axe did good service in cutting away the
rigging and clearing the ship of the wreck.

She immediately righted, drifting helplessly
before the driving storm toward the coast of France.
Having no sail, the vessel refused to answer to her
rudder, and the incessant flashes of lightning
revealed to them the wild surf leaping mountains

high upon the shore to which they were helplessly drifting.

Being more courageous than his fellow-pilgrims, Francisco sought to instill some hope into their breasts; but the monks were insane with fear. Some swooned with fright, and others clung wildly to parts of the vessel so that they could hardly be pulled away. Francisco, with a thought of home and mother and another of heaven, resolved to do all in his power to save his life.

Again were the heavens lighted by that liquid blaze. The wild-eyed passengers and sailors saw that they were frightfully near the shore. At this moment the boom of one of the guns on the after deck thundered forth the signal of danger. Thrice the gun sent its awful message thundering across the waters to the black shores.

One long-continued flash revealed low-lying lands with hills far in the background, a sandy beach in the fore and a small hamlet not half a mile from the beach. It was gone in a moment, and the blackness of despair and raging waters seemed to overwhelm them. With a crash the ship struck ground, and raised such a war of water and sand together, which fell on the main chains, that hopes of safety were abandoned. A wave, striking her on the starboard quarter, pitched her over on her side, and the water, rushing over

the deck, swept away the captain and half the crew. Clinging he knew not how long to the side of the ship highest out of the water, and drenched to the skin by each successive wave, Francisco waited the coming of the angel of death.

"A Flash Revealed an Object Tossing on the Surf."

Anon a flash revealed an object tossing about on the surf. It was a boat, or else he was dreaming. It was a small fisherman's boat in which sat a solitary person, and that person a woman. In a moment it was gone in darkness, and he, the only survivor of the wreck, was ready to believe it a vision of his disordered brain.

But again the lightning came and revealed the boat, propelled certainly by an angelic hand, nearer than before. Could he believe his senses? He was falling into a semi-unconscious state, when a voice from the darkness below shouted from under the lee of the stranded ship. He answered, although the call was in a foreign tongue.

The lightning's flash revealed a small fishing-boat below, in which sat a young girl. Again she called to him in French:

"Monsieur, come, save yourself!"

He tried to descend, but in doing so he fell. He struck some hard substance, and all was a blank.

That reason dawned after such a trial seemed more like magic than reality. All bodily fatigue, all the preoccupation of the mind produced by such terrible events disappeared as they do at the first feeling of sleep. His body seemed to acquire an airy lightness, his perception being brightened in a remarkable manner, his senses redoubled, and the horizon expanded. It was not that gloomy horizon over which alarm had prevailed, but blue, boundless, transparent, with all the charm of a summer sea, and all the spangles of a glorious sun. In the midst of music so clear and sounding, it seemed divine harmony, he saw the low rocky shore as an oasis in the desert, which as he approached resounded with songs, as if some enchanter like Amphion had decreed to attract thither a soul, or build a city.

He seemed lying somewhere on a delightful couch, inspiring the fresh balmy air, like that which may be supposed to reign around the grotto of Circe, formed from such perfumes as set the mind a-dreaming, and such fires as burn the very senses. There floated before him such a vision as had never dawned upon the imagination of man. It was a sylph-like figure, rich in form, with eyes of fascination, smile of love, and bright flowing hair. Phyrne, Cleopatra and Messalina were incomparable to that being, who glided as pure as a ray, like a Christian angel in the midst of Olympus— one of those chaste figures, those calm shadows, those soft visions, which seem to veil the virgin brow of one too pure for this earth.

Wild fantasy slowly gave way to reality, and he found himself lying on a bed, a plain bed at that, in an old, plain room, and through the window he could behold the sea-shore strewn with the wreck of his vessel. It was a disappointing awakening from a delightful vision, but a moment later he was repaid, when a bit of animated sunshine in the form of a lovely girl with great blue eyes and golden hair entered. She saw that his eyes were opened and reason restored, and clasping her hands with joy, a smile on her lovely face, she began to speak in French:

"Is Monsieur' better?"

Fortunately Francisco Estevan understood the language, and made haste to answer that he was better. Then he inquired if any of his companions were saved. A look of sadness came over the sweet face as she answered:

"You should give God thanks for yourself, monsieur; you were the only one who escaped. Many of your companions lie on the beach, and the fishermen of Beaucarre are trying to recover the bodies of the others."

In the sweet young face before him he saw the central object of those delightful visions. Nay, more, he beheld the same form that was revealed by the lightning's flash while he clung to the broken wreck. Mustering up what French he had at his command he asked:

"Did you not rescue me from the wreck last night?"

"Not last night. It has been three days since the awful event."

"Three days, can it be possible?"

"Yes, monsieur, it has been three whole days since the wreck, and you are the only one saved."

4

"Had it not been for you, brave little señorita, I, too, would have found a watery grave." In his earnest gratitude Francisco Estevan seized the small, white hand of his pretty deliverer and kissed it again and again.

She gently withdrew her hand and urged him to keep quiet, as he was still weak and needed rest. She sat at his side and told him all that had transpired since his rescue, and then left him for a few moments to bring some nourishment.

Under the tender care of Hortense De Barre, Francisco Estevan rapidly convalesced, and in a few days was able to get about the hamlet, or wander down to the sea-shore. His young nurse and rescuer nearly always accompanied him, and they grew strongly attached to each other.

A low-browed, scowling youth, with masses of jet-black hair about his face, frequently dogged their footsteps, and more than once Francisco found him eavesdropping.

"Who is he, señorita, who follows us so persistently?" Francisco asked his fair companion, as, one day, strolling on the beach, he caught a glimpse of their shadower behind an old boat.

"He is Monsieur Gyrot," Hortense answered.

"Is he your relative?"

"No, monsieur."

"A friend?"

" An acquaintance," she answered.

Francisco had frequently urged her to tell him her history, but she always declined. All he knew of her was that she was the daughter of a sea-captain from Dieppe, which accounted for her skill in handling the oars in the surf, but further he knew nothing.

"WHO IS HE WHO FOLLOWS US SO PERSISTENTLY?"

Never did Francisco pass a more delightful period than at Beaucarre. Frequently in after years, when amidst the whirlwind and storms of an eventful life, he looked back upon that period as the one green oasis in his existence. He was wholly recovered, and yet he

could not tear himself away from Beaucarre.
Young priest, are you forgetting your vows?
This question, thundered by an ill-tutored conscience, rang in his ear day after day; but, like
persons rushing upon fate, he was blind and deaf
to reason. Being a priest, how could he hope to
wed Hortense, and yet how could he give her up?
She was dearer to him than life, and he was at
times almost ready to say that she would outbal-
ance his salvation.

Love is a plant of quick growth. It matures
and ripens in a day in those genial Southern climes.
Three weeks had elapsed since his recovery, and
the student was almost ready to abandon the
sacerdotal robe for the lily of France. His intended
calling had been kept a secret from all, and Hortense De Barre, the Huguenot, little dreamed that
she had been ministering to a priest. They dis-
cussed almost every subject save religion. For the
last few days John Gyrot had disappeared from
Beaucarre, and they were left quite to themselves.

Francisco would hardly admit, even to himself,
that he was in love. One designed for the priesthood must not love; but this strange, beautiful
French girl, the embodiment of all that was good,
pure, and holy, had enchanted him.

One day Gyrot returned as suddenly as he had
disappeared. His tired, haggard manner and

travel-stained clothing bore evidence of a long journey. He did not immediately address himself to either Hortense or Francisco; but, with a triumphant smile on his face, he kept aloof for a day or two. On the third day, however, as Francisco wandered alone on the beach, his mind filled with those beautiful day-dreams which for weeks had made existence a paradise, Gyrot suddenly approached him and, laying his hand on the student's shoulder, said:

"I want to talk with you, monsieur."

Francisco had no objection, and expressed himself as willing to hear whatever Señor Gyrot might have to say.

"Come under the pines."

The pines were three tall trees growing near the beach above a low bluff of rocks, and thither they went and seated themselves on some stones.

"You are a Spaniard, monsieur."

"I am a Spanish-American. I was born in Cuba."

"You have been studying at Salamanca for the priesthood."

"You have taken needless pains to inform yourself about my private affairs. If that was the object of your recent journey, I could have saved you the trouble had you asked me, for I have nothing to conceal."

"If the monsieur is to be a priest, his attentions to the mademoiselle are not in good taste."

"I understand; you are growing jealous, señor,"

"If monsieur cares nothing for his monastic vows, what will he think when I tell him the mademoiselle is a Huguenot?"

"What!" cried Francisco, leaping to his feet as suddenly as if a mine had been sprung beneath him. Without seeming to notice his confusion, Gyrot, who took a devilish satisfaction in his work, went on:

"The mademoiselle is a Protestant, a hated heretic, a Huguenot. The monsieur has not well informed himself, or he would know that her father, Captain De Barre of the navy, was an own cousin of Coligni."

"Say no more! I care not to hear another word," cried Francisco, and he hurried away from his evil genius. One living in the present age of freedom and enlightenment cannot understand the emotions of rage, shame, remorse, and even fear which tortured the soul of Francisco Estevan. All his education, his superstition and traditions revolted at thought of heresy. He who had advocated the Inquisition and the extermination of heretics by any means had fallen in love with a Huguenot! He who was to become a priest had been infatuated with a heretic.

"I cannot believe it!" he declared, as he walked along the beach, heedless of the malicious grin of his rival. When the first wild tumult of emotion had given way to sober thought, he determined to seek Hortense and learn the truth from her.

"Be she heretic or devil, she will speak the truth," he thought.

It was like wringing the heart from his bosom. Never before had he realized how dear to him the little French girl had grown; but of all crimes, heresy was the greatest. Had she been a murderess, a common thief, or an outcast, penance and prayer would have given her absolution; but for Protestantism there was no cure.

He sought an early interview with Hortense, and found her in the unlovely garden, the only blooming flower in the desolate *plaisance*. She greeted him with a smile, but his face was unusually grave, and she saw that something was wrong.

"What has gone amiss?" she asked.

"Señorita, I have come to talk with you for perhaps the last time."

"Is monsieur going away?" He was quite sure her face expressed sorrow.

"Yes—I shall return to Spain. The señorita knows I am a Spaniard."

"Of course, I have known it all along," she answered.

"Is the señorita a Huguenot?"

She fixed her great, truthful eyes on his face and answered:

"I am."

He leaned against the framework of a vineless arbor and for several moments was like one stunned, while she continued:

"I am a Huguenot, and the monsieur a Catholic; but do we not both bow before the same God? Should not I give him the right to his religious views, and he accord the same to me? My father and my brother were slain in a Catholic riot. I saw their bleeding and mutilated bodies dragged through the streets by men gone mad over religion. They have forgotten the commands of the Master and seem inspired by the spirit of the evil one. They forget: ' This is my commandment, that ye love one another.' When I saw them dragging my dear father's lifeless and mutilated body through the street, I remembered the text: 'They shall put you out of the synagogues; yea, the time cometh that whosoever killeth you, will think that he doeth God service.' * The prophecy is fulfilled. My poor father, so gentle and kind, so brave and noble, was slain like a wild beast; but, monsieur, I bear the Catholics no ill will; they are

---

* JOHN, 16:2.

crazed, they are deceived, and think they do God service. Let us be friends."

She extended her hand to Francisco, who drew back with a shudder, as if it were polluted, and cried:

"No, no! touch me not. No heretics, none who deny the faith; shall pollute me with their unholy touch. Adieu!"

He turned on his heel and left her gazing at him through those beautiful eyes swimming in tears.

The only bright dream of his life was over, and he hastened from the hamlet as if it had been the abode of fiends. He journeyed on foot to a convent where he got transportation to Spain to resume his studies. Love's young dream was past, swallowed in grief and pain, and the student was paler and more melancholy than before.

CHAPTER IV.

THE early explorers on the American continent, each gave new names to rivers, bays, gulfs, and lakes, until the student is apt to become confused in his researches among their chronicles. John Ribault followed the same course, giving to Floridian streams French names as he sailed along the coast, and for a while America had its Seine, its Loire, and its Garonne.

As a class the French are an enthusiastic people, and the idea of a new colony in a new country, of building up a great empire, filled the colonists at Fort Charles with enthusiasm. Albert, the man left in command of Fort Charles, was brave and enterprising, but lacked the power of controlling men in the wilderness where he had not the strong arm of the civil law to aid him. He was an adventurer, and thought more of finding a Mexico or Peru than planting fields of corn. When the more prudent members of the colony advised him to devote more time to agriculture, he was indignant.

"I command here, and I will seek for gold. The paraousties * tell of rich mines of silver and gold."

His was an error common to early colonists. With his emigrants he roved about the country, until provisions failed, powder and ball for their matchlocks gave out, and the Indians would no longer supply their colony. The governor of the colony became intolerant and overbearing, and soon his companions began to take measures to get rid of him. While they were planning a mutiny, he precipitated matters himself by knocking down a young man in a fit of frenzy. The injured party sought revenge and' assassinated Albert the next night. He was not punished for the offence, and historians speak of Albert's death as the act of a revolt on the part of the colony. A more prudent man named Barre was chosen in his stead, and he at once advised a return to France.

"How can we return?" some of the more despondent asked. "We have no vessel."

"Build one," said Barre.

Ribault failing to appear with the promised recruits and supplies for the infant colony, they set to work to build and rig out a vessel. They were almost at death's door, and gaunt famine was staring them in the face. Had they devoted one-

* The term applied to Indian chiefs by French Hugue-nots.

tenth the energy to planting and sowing which they now used to construct a frail bark, it would have placed them above want. Putting to sea in this frail craft they were driven about at the mercy of wind and waves, until their water and provisions were exhausted, and then they had recourse to cannibalism. A remnant of the colony was finally picked up by an English vessel and taken to England, where Raleigh and Queen Elizabeth listened to their strange story of adventures in the New World.

John Ribault had not deserted the infant colony in Florida as they supposed. On his return to France, he found a civil war raging between the theological factions—Roman Catholics and Huguenots—with unrelenting violence. The monarch, the court and, Coligni were all involved in this unfortunate strife.

"I should like to aid you," said Coligni to Ribault's plea for immediate succor for those in the wilds of Florida; "but at present you see we can do nothing."

"If our people were transferred to this goodly land it would put an end to this unholy strife," answered Ribault.

"Very true, monsieur," Coligni answered, "I feel a more personal interest in the cause of the Huguenots now, for my dead cousin's child appeals to me every hour to escape this accursed persecution. Let us wait, hope and pray for better times."

Those better times did not come until 1564, almost two years from the departure of the first colony. Then the regent and her son provided Coligni with money and three armed ships—The *Elizabeth* of Hanfleur, *Petite Britain* and *Falcon.* The little squadron was placed under the command of René Laudonnière, who had accompanied Ribault on his first voyage. He took with him young men of family and fortune, mechanics and laborers, Jacob Le Moyne as artist and geographer of the expedition, and two skillful pilots, the brothers Vasseur of Dieppe.

On learning of the fitting out of the second expedition, Hortense went to her cousin to plead with him to be permitted to go with it. The squadron had sailed before she reached Havre de Grace; but Coligni, who still lingered there, assured her she should go with the next. The hot war of persecution had reached even Beaucarre, and she was compelled to fly that portion of the country. Gyrot had continued his persecutions with cunning audacity and persistance. He urged her to wed him, assuring her of protection if she did and death if she did not, until her choice seemed to be marriage with that monster or death at the stake.

Gyrot, by his cunning and duplicity, managed to keep on the best terms with both Protestants and Romanists. How he succeeded was a mystery to Hortense. She never asked him. She avoided him as she would a monster. Just before the departure of the second colony under Laudonnière, . Gyrot suddenly disappeared from the neighborhood where the brave girl was staying; but she did not suspect that he had gone to America. Day by day she anticipated seeing his ugly face and feeling more keenly some devilish plan he had set on foot. Coligni, assuring the unhappy girl she should be sent to America as soon as practicable, placed her with some friends powerful enough to protect her from both Romanists and Gyrot.

Since her meeting with Francisco Estevan the girl was overwhelmed with woe. Those sad, burning eyes seemed ever gazing at her, and his deep solemn voice rang in her ears. Gyrot, in a fit of exultation, had told her that Estevan was an unrighteous priest whose chief desire was to burn her at the stake.

"He may be a priest," she answered, "but he is not a bad man. He has a heart in his breast which beats as tenderly as may be found in a Luther or Melancthon."

It will be necessary in this chapter to follow the fortunes of Laudonnière. He set sail from Havre de Grace the 22d of April, 1564, and, after a prosperous voyage, arrived at Florida on the 22d of June. Unknown to Hortense or any of her friends, John Gyrot had gone with the expedition, intending to be in the new colony when Mademoselle De Barre should arrive there, and hoping in the New World to succeed better in his courtship than he had in the Old. Landing in Florida, Laudonnière was met by one of the Floridian princes, named Saturiova, who almost worshipped him. Bringing his two sons to the French, Saturiova through an interpreter said:

"These are my sons, both of whom are great warriors and will fight for the Frenchmen."

The eldest, an amiable young man, became very fond of the French, instructing them in the state of the country, their friends and enemies, and everything they would have to fear. Laudonnière, without regarding Fort Charles, by the advice of Saturiova fixed his residence on the river May, and engaged the paraousti or chief to accompany him in an excursion up the river.

They had proceeded but a little way when Laudonnière ordered a halt and pitched his tent.

"Are you going to remain here?" asked Ottigny, one of his officers.

"Yes, I will send you with D'Erlac higher up the stream to make discoveries."

They were accordingly sent in company with
Saturiova up the river while Laudonnière awaited
their return in his tent. He displayed more mili-
tary genius than his predecessors, and came early
to regard the Indians as unreliable and treacherous.
At the end of seven days Ottigny and D'Erlac
returned.

"What have you discovered?" Laudonnière
asked.

"A chief two hundred and fifty years old,"
D'Erlac answered.

Laudonnière, with a look of incredulity, asked:
"Have you discovered nothing else?"

"A goodly country, vast in extent, with famous
rivers and lakes and covered with the most dense
forest I ever saw."

"Have you found no cities?"

"No, we discovered only villages; but we heard
of great cities further inland."

"Have you found no mines of gold or silver?"
Laudonnière early became infected with the fever
for gold, a disease which had excited the Spaniards
to such deeds of cruelty. D'Erlac answered:

"We have found no mines; but Saturiova
assures us there are mines rich in gold and silver."

"Where?"

"Not in his country, but in the distant land
governed by one Timagoa, who is his enemy, and

if you will assist him in subduing this foe, he will give you all the gold and silver in that country."

Laudonnière at once sent for Saturiova, and that cunning savage hurried to the tent of the French commandant. Saturiova was a shrewd politician if not a great general. His design had been, from the first, to secure these powerful allies with their invincible arms to aid him in defeating his enemy Timagoa. He entered the presence of Laudonnière with many protestations of love and friendship.

"Can you tell me where I will find the mines of gold and silver?" asked the Frenchman.

"It is the product of a distant land governed by Timagoa," the wily chief answered. "Timagoa is a very bad man, and if the French with their thunder guns will go with me to subdue him, I will give all the gold and silver to the white men. I only want my revenge on Timagoa."

The principal small-arm of the French at that day was what was called the matchlock, an improvement over the old-fashioned arquebus, the first musket. The wheel-lock had been invented, but had not yet come into general use. The matchlock was a gun with a pan in which was the priming powder connecting with the powder in the barrel by means of a touch-hole. This pan could be opened by a spring. It was fired by a matchcord, which was usually carried in the hand lighted

5

at both ends. A single match-cord would burn for hours. To fire the gun, the match was blown so as to remove the dead ashes, then the pan opened and the match applied to the priming. The gun was heavy and unwieldy, so that, like the arquebus, it was fired from a rack or rest, a rod underneath it. These arms, clumsy as they may seem in these modern days, were very formidable to the Indians.

Laudonnière promised the chief his support; but, after carefully considering the matter, concluded that he could not afford to plunge his young colony into a civil war, and decided to discover the mines without the aid of the cunning Saturiova. He counselled with D'Erlac and asked him what he thought of the plan.

"It is best, monsieur. We should avoid a war with any of these people. I have heard that Timagoa is a very powerful chief, and is disposed to be friendly with us. We have had no quarrel with him, and he may give us the mines without fighting for them."

That night Laudonnière decamped without taking Saturiova into his confidence and sailed up another river, where he met the chief of the province, his wife and four daughters, who hospitably entertained him. Among the presents the French commandant received was a small ball of silver, which confirmed him in the belief that he was in the neighborhood of rich mines. Assembling his men near the mouth of May River, he said:

"We have reached a goodly country surrounded by friendly savages and near mines rich in silver and gold. The soil is rich, yielding its fruits without labor, and I deem it a location fit for the founding of our colony."

All consented, and next day the squadron was ordered to repair to the mouth of May River,* and they commenced the construction of that fort which was to be bathed in innocent blood—Fort Carolinia. Saturiova, the chief, came to them and was so well pleased that he sent Indians to assist in the construction of the fort. The Indians also brought them gold, silver, and pearls, which Laudonnière ordered to be put in the common stock.

As soon as Fort Carolinia was built, Laudonnière dispatched one of his ships to France for recruits and supplies. It now began to look as if the French had taken posesssion of the New World in earnest. Day by day the echoes of the woodman's axe and the thundering crash of falling trees announced that the hand of industry had begun to make the wilderness bloom. Houses were erected beyond the fort, and a future city projected.

---

* Now St. John.

Ottigny was indefatigable in his search for gold and silver. On his return from one expedition, one of his soldiers brought with him several pounds of silver. On seeing it, Laudonnière asked the soldier:

"Where did you get it?"

"From an Indian."

"Where do the Indians get it?"

"Truth, I cannot tell, monsieur."

"Don't they know?"

"This savage got it from another, and he from still another, so that we are unable to trace the metal to its true discoverer."

"Don't they know?"

"If they do, they skillfully conceal the knowledge from us, monsieur. They disagree among themselves as to the direction of the mines, though all say they are a great way off. One paraousti says that off to the north is a mountain of yellow iron, by which he of course means a mountain of gold."

"The dogs are deceiving us," said Laudonnière.

"Saturiova will call on the commandant in the morning. Question him concerning the mountain of gold," said Ottigny.

"That I will."

Accordingly, on the morrow, Saturiova called on Laudonnière. His manner was quiet and dignified, but there was a perceptible coolness on the part of the chief, rather remarkable in one who had been so amiable. This was more marked from the fact that his army of five hundred fighting men were all mustered near the fort, as if to engage in some warlike expedition.

"What has the paraousti to say this morning?" asked Laudonnière.

"I came to remind the white chief of his promise to be the friend of my friends, and the enemy of my enemies! I am ready now to march with my army against Timagoa; will the white chief go with me?"

For a moment Laudonnière was nonplussed. Being a shrewd diplomat he knew it would never do to arouse the hostility of the paraousti in whose territory he believed the famous gold mountain to exist. After a moment's reflection, he answered:

"My presence is necessary here among my people. Our fort is not yet built, and our houses are incomplete, and I dare not leave at present."

"Has my white brother forgotten his promise?"

"No, but I dare not go. My duty to my people demand my presence here for several months yet."

Saturiova, displeased with the refusal, set out with his own army to war. His campaign was so well planned that he succeeded in punishing and humbling his enemy, putting many to the sword, and bringing away twenty-four captives.

When Laudonnière heard of the victory he determined to profit by it. He sent to Saturiova congratulating him on his victory and demanding two of his prisoners whom he designed to send back to Timagoa, and thus gain his friendship. His astonishment can be imagined better than described at the return of D' Erlac with the information that Saturiova absolutely refused to comply with his demand.

"Refuse me! Does the red dog dare refuse me?" cried Laudonnière. "I will humble that proud savage or run him through with my sword."

Summoning forty men with breast-plates, helmets, matchlocks, and swords, he set out to pay Saturiova a visit. Reaching his cabin he left his men at the door, and entered the presence of the chief.¯

"Where are your prisoners?" he demanded.

"What right has my white brother to demand my prisoners? He would not accompany me according to promise," Saturiova answered indignantly.

"I have come for the prisoners," Laudonnière answered, calmly but firmly, "and have brought my soldiers with swords and guns to enforce my request. Where are they?"

Saturiova saw the cavalier draw his glittering sword from its sheath, and began to tremble.

"They became alarmed at the approach, of the white men, and fled to the woods," he answered.

"You have lied," thundered Laudonnière. Then he ordered a search to be made for them, and seized the chief. Two prisoners were brought and turned over to them; whom Laudonnière gave in charge of D' Erlac and L'Vascar to carry to Timagoa. This occurred the 20th of August, 1564, and on the 21st a most terrible hurricane swept over the country, leveling forests and destroying Indian cabins. The clouds were charged with thunder and lightning, and slight earthquake shocks shook the country.

The French were frightened as well as the Indians, but they had sufficient presence of mind not to show their fear, and Laudonnière shrewdly informed the savages that the storm was sent on account of their stubborn perverseness in refusing to give up the prisoners. The thunder he declared to be the great guns of his angry God.

Saturiova gave up all the prisoners, fled from his domain, and it was two months before he returned.

On the 10th of September, D'Erlac and Vasseur set out with the captives under ten men and a sergeant; and, having delivered up their charge to

Timagoa, thereby winning his friendship, proceeded according to instructions from Laudonnière to the province of Outina, the powerful cacique who was supposed to possess full knowledge of the mountain of gold. IIis residence was 127 miles from Fort Carolina, and the road was through an interminable wilderness of swamps and streams.

Outina joyfully received them, and as he was just ready to set out on an expedition against his enemy named Potanou, he invited D'.Erlac to accompany him. Thus the French, despite all their shrewdness, found themselves drawn into an Indian quarrel. It would not do to offend so powerful a chief by a refusal, and, with half his escort, D' Erlac consented to go, sending the other half back to Fort Carolinia for instructions as to how he should act toward this chief.

Outina's army was small, yet with the six Frenchmen armed with those terrible guns, he hoped to defeat his powerful enemy. On the second day's march, they came upon a plain where they found the army of Potanou drawn up in battle array. They so greatly outnumbered the forces of Outina that he was quite in despair.

"We cannot fight against such odds," said the chief to D'Erlac. "We shall be forced to fly for our lives."

"Have no fears," said D'Erlac. "I will save

you. Can you make out the person of Pota-nou?"

"Yes."

"Which is he?"

"The large chief with red and green feathers, and a mantle on his arm."

D'Erlac asked no more, for the princely bearing and dignity of the chief told him who he was.

The smoke issuing from the match-cord indi-cated that the match was lighted. D'Erlac drew up the Indians in battle array, placed his men with matchlocks ready to pour in a volley at a given signal, and advanced a few paces. Unfastening the rod under the barrel of his gun, he set the rest. Then he carefully blew the match to free it of dead ashes, and opened the pan. The Indians on both sides stood gazing on this strange ceremony with amazement, not comprehending what it meant. Even Potanou, at whose breast the gun was aimed, was as much lost in wonder as the others. There was a flash, a stunning report, and the chief fell, shot through the heart. A moment later a rattling crash of fire-arms from the other Frenchmen put the savages to flight, and Outina pursued them with great slaughter.

Soon after this signal victory, D'Erlac was recalled to Fort Carolina by Laudonnière, who was displeased at his taking any part in the war between Outina and Potanou, especially as they were having some internal trouble in the colony.

Thus we find the persecuted who had come to the New World to find homes and peace, plunged by their own violence into strife which was to grow more and more bitter until their old enemy should come and sweep them from the face of the earth.

CHAPTER V.

UNDER certain circumstances it is an easy matter to change men from saints to devils. A single mischief-breeding person may ruin a community of people who otherwise would have lived in peace and respectability. John Gyrot soon became the evil genius of the colony. As he grew older, he became more cunning and more mischievous. He soon learned that discontent existed among the volunteers of the expedition, who were gentlemen and totally unfit for this service. They complained that they were not as well treated as laborers; nor did they deserve to be, for they were worth little or nothing to the community. They were consumers without producing and were useless. Laudonnière was not slow to understand that the life and vitality of the colony depended on the laborers and men who were willing to till the soil, and consequently he was not slow to show his favor to them. Secretly circulating among the idlers, Gyrot sought to augment rather than allay

75

the difficulties. He was cunning enough to keep himself well in the background, so as not to bring censure upon himself. Matters had reached a high state of discontent when Laudonnière ordered D'Erlac, in whom he had the greatest confidence, home. One cause of dissatisfaction in the colony was lack of a clergyman to perform divine service; but their greatest grievance was a dearth of provisions and a near prospect of famine.

"Why longer stay in this wilderness and starve," urged John Gyrot to a band of secret conspirators. "Let us put Laudonnière out of the way and return to France, or put ourselves in charge of the colony."

It was Gyrot's plan either to destroy the colony or to get his friends in control before the arrival of Hortense De Barre.

The seeds of dissension once sown took root and brought forth fruit in a well-laid conspiracy to take the life of Laudonnière. One of the conspirators was discovered and hanged, and Laudonnière ordered a ship-load of malcontents to be sent to France. As they were going aboard the vessel, the commandant approached Gyrot.

"You can return, also," he said.

"I return, monsieur?" cried Gyrot in well-feigned surprise. "I am the most faithful of the colonists, why should I return?"

"Do you not wish to go to France?"

"I do not, monsieur."

"Then complain no more of the country and your usage."

"I beg the monsieur's pardon—there is some mistake, for I have made no complaint. I am the commandant's warmest friend. I love the colony."

The hypocritical pretenses of John Gyrot so deceived Laudonnière that when' he dispatched some of the malcontents, who still remained, under Roche Ferriere to complete the discovery of Outina's canton, the wily Gyrot was left behind with Ottigny and D'Erlac as a personal body-guard of the commandant.

One day John Gyrot came upon three of the discontented gentlemen in a building where they had met to brood over their hard fate. They were Stephen, a Genevois, Des Fourneaux, and La Croix, . Frenchmen.

"Why do you linger here in this poor country," said Gyrot,- "where starvation must ultimately sweep us all off the earth. There is a golden conquest open for us."

"Where?" asked the malcontents.

"Every ship leaving the West Indies is laden with gold and precious stones. The Spaniards are Catholics and make war on Protestants. France is almost on the point of war with Spain. We have ships, guns, and brave men, why not sail to the West Indies and there reap our fortune? There are heaps and mountains of gold already dug and refined, without our risking our lives and health here in the wilderness."

In those three Gyrot found eager listeners to his plan, and he continued in the same strain to point out the cruelty of the Spaniards toward the natives, whom they had slain by millions, while millions more were suffering in bondage. Would they not be wholly justified in thus seeking revenge.

The words of Gyrot sank deep into the minds of his hearers. Vengeance is always sweet, but when seasoned with a golden reward it becomes irresistible. After a few moments, Des Fourneaux said:

"I will go if we can get men to join us."

"You can," continued Gyrot. "But mention the matter to the men and you will have all the followers you desire. Besides, we can prevail on Laudonnèire to sign a commission for our cruising upon the Spaniards in the Gulf of Mexico."

The plan was agreed upon, and while Gyrot seemed loyal to Laudonnière, he was kept posted on all the movements of the mutineers. Stephens, Des Fourneaux, and La Croix were desperate men, and the idea of piracy being more acceptable to them than a life of hardship and trial, they gathered about them sixty soldiers and sailors, the worst

JOHN GYROT BETRAYING LAUDONNIÈR TO THE PIRATES.

in the colony, and proceeded to lay their plans for plundering the Spanish.

At this time Laudonnière was ill from a fever contracted in the swamps, and unable to leave his bed. Gyrot, by skillful manipulations, became his only attendant, and Ottigny and D'Erlac were sent away. It was night and the cabin of Laudonnière was dimly lighted with a single wax taper. Gyrot was at the bedside of the sick commandant, when the tramping of feet without reached their ears. Laudonnière was alarmed at 'the sounds.

"See who approaches, Monsieur Gyrot," he exclaimed.

Glancing from the door, Gyrot, in feigned alarm, answered:

"Messieurs Stephens, Des Fourneaux, and La Croix, with a large party of armed men."

"It is a conspiracy, Gyrot. I feared as much. Draw your sword and we will defend our lives." Ill as he was, Laudonnière leaped from his bed and seized his sword. It had been arranged that Gyrot should make a show of defence, but both were speedily disarmed and Laudonnière plundered of all his effects. He was then carried on board a vessel lying in the river and ordered to sign the commission for them to cruise against the Spanish.

"I cannot," said the commandant. "Such an act would be piracy."

"They make war on Protestants," argued Des Fourneaux, "and we intend to make war on them. Sign the commission."

"I will not."

"Sign or die." Des Fourneaux held a dagger at his throat threatening his life if he did not sign the commission. Laudonnière seized the pen.

"Bear witness that I do this under duress," he said. He then signed the document and, handing it to them, added, "Take it, it is your death warrant that I have signed."

They went away, and, according to arrangements, took John Gyrot with them. They embarked on board the two new vessels, and set sail on the 8th of December, intending to plunder Yaguana.

Before they left the river May, they disputed among themselves, and the two vessels separated, one steering for the isle of Cuba, and the other, which was never heard from, for the Lucayan islands. The vessel steering for Cuba chose D'Oranger captain, and a bolder, more cruel pirate could not have been selected.

The crew was now fairly embarked on their terrible career. In those days the Spaniards were themselves little better than robbers. Cortez and Pizarro were licensed pirates who operated on a grand scale, so these Frenchmen found an excuse for retaliating on them.

On the fifth day after leaving the river May, the look-out at the masthead discovered a sail. The announcement caused no little speculation on board the pirate ship. D'Oranger, coming up from below, mounted the rigging and with his glass swept the waters. At first the stranger was so far away they could not make her out; but changing their course they bore down upon her. The pirates crowded the deck in order to get a better view of her, and the air was full of speculations. At last the look-out from the masthead hailed the captain on deck with the joyful announcement:

"I have her nationality."

"What is she?" D'Oranger asked.

"A Spanish brigantine, headed for Cuba or San Domingo."

The shout of joy which went up from the deck was somewhat checked by D' Oranger, who said:

"Ships from Spain do not carry gold."

"But this vessel may have provisions on board, which are much more acceptable to starving men," Des Fourneaux answered.

They crowded all sail, and the Spanish ship, not realizing her danger, held steadily on her course. The lombards or cannon in the forward deck were gotten in readiness, and the men armed with battle

6

axes, pikes, and matchlocks. They bore down
to within three-fourths of a mile of the brigantine,
and, firing a gun, hoisted the French ensign.

The brigantine's people were amazed and
alarmed. They seemed not to think of resistance so
much as flight. The vessel was put about on her
best sailing point and sped away with every stitch
of canvas she was able to carry, while the determined Frenchmen pressed on in pursuit.

Francisco Estevan was aboard the Spanish
brigantine. He was on his return to Cuba, summoned by the sudden illness of his mother. Francisco had not yet entered the order of the priesthood, and was only a pale, thoughtful student, on
whose face there seemed to rest the shadow of a
great sorrow, which prayers and tears failed to
relieve. This shadow had followed him since his
abrupt departure from Beaucarre. The sweet face,
golden hair, and blue eyes of the fair Huguenot continually haunted him. His ancient traditions,
superstitions, even the sacredness of his intended
calling could not overcome the spell produced by
this sweet Christian spirit. Her resignation touched
his soul and at times he almost thought, down deep
in his heart, that the persecution of her family
was the work of the devil.

For one reason or another Francisco had failed
to be ordained, until we find him on his way home

without having taken the preliminary steps toward donning the sacerdotal robe. He took passage at Seville, and, so far, the voyage had been prosperous. The brigantine, in addition to a goodly cargo of wine, provisions, and cloth goods for the West India trade, had a number of passengers, men, women, and children, aboard.

Francisco was in the forward part of the ship when the pursuer was discovered. There was much speculation as to her strange conduct; but no serious fears were entertained until a wreath of white smoke curled up from her forecastle and a ball came skipping over the water, accompanied by the distant boom of a cannon. As the fine spray clipped from the crested waves by the round shot flew over the deck, the captain of the brigantine became fully aroused to the danger of his situation. He displayed the Spanish flag, put his vessel about, and bore away as we have stated with every stitch of canvas spread. Francisco, who had been dreaming his day-dream, in which were blue eyes, golden hair, and a fair face, turned from the forward deck and hurried aft to see if they would be pursued.

" What does it mean, captain?" he asked.

" We are chased by a pirate," was the answer.

" Can we escape her?"

" She gains on us."

Francisco became fully aroused to their danger, and the spirit of the warrior, so natural in him, began to assert itself. He insisted that they arm themselves and beat off the pirate; but, alas! they were deficient in both arms and courage. While still discussing the trying situation, another puff of smoke issued from the forecastle of the pursuer, and there came a loud crash as an iron ball struck the stern, coming through to the poop deck, and, spinning half-way across, struck a coil of rope and rolled along the deck.

The passengers and most of the crew were wild with fear, uttering the most piteous cries and prayers. Finding escape impossible, the captain caused his ship to heave to and struck his colors. The Frenchmen came boldly alongside, and D'Oranger, Des Fourneaux, La Croix, Stephens, John Gyrot, and their grim followers, with swords in hand, poured over the side of the prize. Francisco Estevan, who stood on the high poop deck biting his lips with indignation at this humiliating surrender, started with a cry of astonishment on discovering John Gyrot among his captors.

"I need expect no mercy now," the young Spaniard thought.

The male prisoners were driven forward, and their hands tied behind their backs, while the women and children were sent below. Then the

pirates began plundering the ship of its valuables.
D'Oranger prudently placed a guard over the
liquors, and permitted only a limited amount to
be issued to his men. Then followed a long consultation as to what should be done with the prisoners. The sun went down, the moon rose, and
night had resumed her .sway before the question
was decided.

Francisco Estevan stood in the forecastle, his
hands tied behind his back gazing at the broad
faced, friendly moon riding peacefully in the
heavens, and asked himself how it was all to end.
Would he live to see the dawn of another day, or
would those dark monsters put an end to his
sufferings that night? Mingled with the sad
recollections of the past and the gloomy reflections
of the present, was the sweet face of the pretty
Huguenot, which he could not banish from his
memory. He was standing, gloomy and silent,
among the other prisoners, when John Gyrot
approached him.

"Monsieur Estevan, the priest, did you think
I would not know you?"

Francisco glanced at the ugly face surmounted by
a mass of black hair, but made no answer. With
a gleam of satisfaction on his diabolical features,
Gyrot added:

"Monsieur does not seem happy."

"No, the sight of a reptile is not inspiring."

"Monsieur is not complimentary; but, considering his present condition, I will overlook what he says. Why did he so suddenly leave Beaucarre?"

"I had no wish to stay longer."

"Monsieur found the society of the Huguenot, Mademoiselle De Barre, delightful."

There was such a tantalizing tone in the ironical words of the Frenchman that the blood of the Spaniard was fired and had he been free he would have struck him.

"Don't breathe her name—hypocrite—you are not worthy!" gasped Francisco.

With a low, disagreeable chuckle, which, like his speech, seemed choked in the throat of the pirate, Gyrot turned away and left the prisoner.

The forlorn group of captives silently wondered what would be their fate. The moon now riding high in the heavens, flooded the sea with peaceful light. The captors were busy arranging something, and it was several moments before the captives could comprehend their designs. They brought a broad plank, and, placing one end of it over the side of the vessel, lashed the other end firmly to the bulwark. When the prisoners realized their fate a storm of wails and groans went up from them. Some even fell on their knees and implored their captors to spare their lives; but the

Frenchmen, without heeding their entreaties, went coolly about their abominable work. When the board had been made steady, D'Oranger directed his men to bring a prisoner, and Stephens and La Croix seized the trembling master of the prize and dragged the wretched Spaniard to the plank.

"Place him on it."

The prisoner struggled, and they had to prick him with the points of their swords to drive him forward. His hands were securely tied behind his back, and in this manner he was made to walk to the end of the board and jump off into the sea, his drowning screams piercing the ears of his wretched companions like a knife.

"Bring on another," commanded the pirate captain.

A second one was brought and, after a desperate struggle, placed on the board. He implored and prayed to be spared, but was unrelentingly pushed forward at the points of their swords, until he bled from a score of wounds. Goaded to madness, he rushed forward and plunged into the sea, never to rise. Thus the horrible work went on. One by one the cries and supplications of the captives were hushed as their numbers grew less. Without a murmur, Francisco Estevan awaited his summons to death. He strove in vain to burst the cords which bound his wrists, determined to sell his life like a soldier; but no human strength

unaided could
burst t h o s e
cords. At last
a pirate seized his shoulder.
"Monsieur, your time
has come," he said. Francisco made no resistance,

" ' WALK ! ' YELLED THE
PIRATES AT LAST."

and was led like a bullock

to the slaughter. There was a short ladder leading to the board.

"Mount!" cried D'Oranger.

La Croix and Stephens, with drawn swords, stood
ready to drive him to his fate. Turning on the
pirate crew a calm look, the young Spaniard said:
"You will receive your reward for this work."
Then he mounted the ladder.

On the fatal plank, he paused a moment to murmur a last prayer and close his eyes forever on the
world. The Frenchmen realized by his proud, defiant manner that he was superior to ordinary vic-
tims, and he was given a few moments to pray. It
was an age of heartless cruelty, and yet even the
pirates believed in prayer.

"Walk! or we will push you from the board!"
yelled the pirates at last.

Taking one step, Francisco paused, and, with
his eyes raised toward heaven, cried:

"Hortense!"

At this moment some one ran forward from the
after part of the ship.

"Hold! Captain D'Oranger, that prisoner must
be spared."

Francisco very naturally turned his eyes toward
the speaker, and to his amazement discovered that
it was John Gyrot, his enemy.

"Monsieur Gyrot, have you lost your senses?"

asked D'Oranger. "Dead men tell no tales, and if we put them all to the bottom of the sea, we shall have nothing to fear."

"I claim the prisoner for myself. He has just spoken a name which reveals a secret."

Though all had heard the name "Hortense," none could understand its import.

"Is it your design to give the prisoner his liberty?" asked D'Oranger.

"No, I reserve him for a greater punishment than you could inflict."

The wicked eyes of John Gyrot, gleaming with hate, bore evidence to the truth of his assertion. He addressed a few words in an undertone to D'Oranger and La Croix, and the prisoner was taken from the board. This interruption had caused a little flurry of excitement among the pirates. Estevan was hurried aboard the French vessel, was strongly ironed and thrust into the hold.

"The monsieur can thank me for his deliverance," said Gyrot, putting his ugly face in at the door.

Francisco made no answer, and, with a mocking jest about the ingratitude of some people, Gyrot left him. Francisco in his gloomy prison passed a miserable night, and sometimes he almost wished he had been plunged into the sea with the others. At intervals throughout the night he imagined he could hear the shriek and splash as some unfortunate was driven from the plank into the sea. Before long other sounds reached his ears—the sounds of transferring the cargo to the pirate ship.

Dawn came. The worn-out prisoner had just sunk into a light slumber, when he was startled by the distant boom of a cannon and the hurried tramp of feet above. He sat up and listened. Above, everything seemed in a state of confusion, and he rightly conjectured that a Spanish man-of-war was about to attack the pirate. The prisoner began to hope.

CHAPTER VI.

THE anxiety of Francisco Estevan at that moment was indescribable. At one time he thought the pursuer of the pirate must be near; but the next boom of the cannon assured him she was falling astern. In his dungeon he could form no opinion save by sounds and the motion of the vessel. By the creaking of cordage above and the plunging motion of the ship, he knew the pirate was under way.

How was all this to end, and what was to be his fate? he asked himself. Gyrot had not reserved him for any humane motive; but his fate could not be more terrible than the one from which his enemy had snatched him. In his imagination he could see the bones of his former companions imbedded among the sea-weeds, the crabs crawling through their fleshless ribs, the fishes eating out their eyes, while the eternal tides rolled them hither and thither giving no rest.

With such horrifying pictures he fed his fancy

as time wore on and all signs of pursuit died away. At last some one came down the companion ladder; he had not been forgotten after all.

A lantern shone in his face and by the rays he recognized Gyrot.

"Has the monsieur enjoyed himself?" Gyrot asked with a hypocritical smile.

"Were we pursued?" Francisco asked.

"Yes."

"Does the pursuer gain on us?"

"No, monsieur, I am happy to inform you that the man-of-war has fallen too far astern for us to suffer any uneasiness from her. I came to bring the monsieur to the deck."

Gyrot waited as if expecting some expression of gratitude from the prisoner; but Francisco was silent.

"Does the monsieur care to go on deck?" he asked.

"I do not care to remain in the dark, musty hold of the ship," Francisco answered. "You need not fear me escaping, as I am only one against many. Can you remove these irons?"

"Yes, monsieur; I beg pardon for not having noticed them before. I shall be very happy to give the monsieur his liberty." There was something hypocritical in the soft easy tones of Gyrot. Estevan shuddered at the cold touch of his hands.

Gyrot's face was habitually pale, his hands cold
and clammy, and his manner that of a vampire. He
had no virtue save persistency, knew no art save
cunning, and worshipped no God save selfish
desire.

Never did one man hate another more than John
Gyrot hated Estevan; yet his deceitful nature
evinced a hypocritical affection for the man he
hated, for he could be nothing if not a hollow sham.
Gyrot could not even hate as other men did. He
removed the shackles, and Francisco followed him
to the deck, where he gazed about over the water
to see if the pursuer were in sight. Far in their
wake a speck could be seen on the horizon, which
was doubtless· the man-of-war. A fourth of a
mile on their larboard was the prize, aboard
which was D'Oranger and a part of the French
crew.

Des Fourneaux was in command of the pirate.

The Frenchmen were quiet and orderly, yet
desperate. Francisco very much wished to know
the fate of the others of his ship, especially the
women and children, but he dared not ask.
Though he was given the freedom of the deck, he
observed that he was closely watched.

Des Fourneaux at last approached him, and, with
the politeness characteristic of his nation, asked:

"Does monsieur speak French?"

"I do," the prisoner answered.

"Very good; we shall get along better; how is monsieur?"

"As well as a captive whose fate is unknown can be."

"Where was monsieur bound?"

"Cuba."

"Is monsieur a priest?"

"No; I am a student."

"To become a priest?"

"Who informed you?"

"Monsieur Gyrot met you at Beaucarre?"

"Gyrot is correct—we met at Beaucarre."

"Monsieur is then a priest?"

Francisco shook his head.

"No; I have not yet taken the vows. Señor, may I ask you what my fate is to be?"

For a moment there was a troubled expression on the Frenchman's face; then he evasively answered:

"Monsieur Gyrot, your friend, saves you."

Estevan knew that the friendship of Gyrot was mockery, and the information he received did not tend in the least to elevate his spirits. The day passed without any incident worthy of mention. Evening came and Francisco was alone in the forecastle when he noticed a man approaching him. It was too dark to make out his features, and at first he thought it was Gyrot; but as the man drew nearer, he discovered that it was not Gyrot. He came quite close to Estevan, glancing carefully about as if he did not wish to be seen. When at the Spaniard's side he said in an undertone:

"Does monsieur speak French?"

This was twice he had been asked if he spoke French.

"I do," he answered.

"Don't be discouraged, monsieur. I may be able to save you."

"Who are you?" Francisco asked.

"Trenchant, the pilot of this unfortunate expedition."

"Then you, too, are a pirate."

"Not of my own free will."

"Did you come from Florida?"

"I did, monsieur. We are a part of the colony planted there by Laudonnière. These pirates are made up of soldiers and adventurers who should never have been permitted to go to the New World. They robbed Laudonnière, and, with a dagger at his throat, forced him to sign a commission to cruise against the Spaniards. I was forced to come; but, as soon as I can, I am going to run away and return to Florida."

"You took no part in the terrible work last night?"

"No, monsieur, God forbid I should do anything so monstrous! We must not talk longer, monsieur, or I may be discovered, for I also am a prisoner."

Francisco, realizing that he had met a friend, grasped his hand.

"One word, señor, before you go. Will you help me to escape?"

"I will aid you with my life if need be, monsieur."

"Are you a Catholic?"

"I WILL AID YOU WITH MY LIFE."

"No, a Huguenot; but what does it matter, if one be honest and of the same great family. We worship the same God, though we have different creeds. We are menaced by a common danger; let us be brothers."

"We will!"

Estevan warmly embraced the Huguenot, and,

7

strange to say, realized the joy of an approving conscience in accepting the friendship of even a heretic.

"Answer a few questions, and we will separate."

"What are they?" I shall keep back nothing,"
said Trenchant.

"Do you know whither we are bound?"

"We are steering toward the western port of
Hispaniola, where they intend to careen the prize
as she is leaking."

"Where will they then go?"

"Probably to Cuba."

"When they touch at Cuba, we will escape."

"Would not my escape be like leaping from
the frying-pan into the fire?"

"Why?"

"I would fall into the hands of the Spaniards,
who would burn me as a Huguenot or hang me as a
pirate."

"No, no," Estevan quickly replied. "My
father has great influence with the governor of
Cuba. You need have no fear of harm."

Trenchant said he must go, and the young men
separated. The pirates reached the western port
of Hispaniola, where in a harbor near Yaguana they
careened their leaky prize, and, after scraping and
recaulking it, steered toward Baracoa in the island
of Cuba, where they captured a richly laden Spanish caravel of fifty or sixty tons burthen. The

pirates inspired the West Indies with dread, and commerce, which had already become considerable in this part of the New World, was greatly crippled. The pirates held toward Hispaniola, and near Cape Tiberane took a patache richly laden, on board of which was the governor of Jamaica, which island was then in possession of the Spaniards. Two of the governor's sons were also made captives.

D'Oranger, as bold and enterprising as the buccaneers who followed him a century later, retained the prisoners on board his prize and demanded a ransom for them. The shrewd governor determined to outwit the pirate, and the amount of the ransom was agreed upon, and the pirates, with two vessels, stood over toward Jamaica.

Francisco Estevan was retained on the French ship and not permitted to communicate with the governor. D'Oranger, with a part of the pirates, had the governor on board the patache.

The governor wrote a letter to his wife asking her to send by his eldest son, who was to be the bearer of the message, the amount of gold required for his ransom, and showing it to D'Oranger asked:

"Will that do, señor?"

"It will, and when the ransom comes, you shall soon have your liberty."

As the son departed to secure the ransom for

his father, the governor slipped another note, of
quite a different import, into the hand of the youth.
The young Spaniard was shrewd enough not to
evince by word or sign that he had received the
missive, and did not open it until he was among
friends safe on shore.   The message secretly
placed in his hand by his father read:

"Do not send any ransom, but notify the officers of the
navy and have an armed force sent at midnight, sufficient
to capture the pirates at dawn of day."

These instructions were carried out.   The pirate
ships lay near the island in safe mooring awaiting
the ransom which was to come next morning.
Francisco found himself so closely guarded by
Gyrot, La Croix, and Des Fourneaux that escape
was impossible.

At dawn of day the harbor was startled by the
booming of cannon, and three Spanish vessels of
superior burthen bore down upon them.   It was
evident from the first how the conflict would end,
and both the pirate ships attempted flight; but the
chain-shot from the Spanish vessel so cut and
crippled the rigging and sails of D'Oranger's ship
that it could not be successfully worked, and
was carried by the board.   The pirates who were
not cut down in the fight soon paid the penalty
of their crime by swinging at the yard-arm.

The other ship, on which Estevan was detained prisoner, and of which Trenchant was pilot, escaped, and, proving swifter than the Spanish vessels, soon set pursuit at defiance. On board this vessel were twenty-five Frenchmen, all that were left from the original number, among whom were John Gyrot, Stephens the Genevois, Des Fourneaux, and La Croix. They owed their lives to the skill of Trenchant their pilot, whom they both hated and feared, but whose services were indispensable. The management of the vessel being entirely in his control he steered for the Bahama islands.

Trenchant ascertained that most of the men were heartily tired of this mode of life and willing to return to Florida, save the ringleaders, who had good reason to dread the vegeance of Laudonnière. When a vote was taken to return a stormy scene ensued, and Gyrot, Des Fourneaux, La Croix, and Stephens bitterly opposed it; but Trenchant was cool and determined. He placed himself in control and declared he would steer the vessel to May River, and if the objectors interposed any obstacle to his design, he would put them in irons. The will of the majority prevailed and the ship sailed for the May River.

As soon as he could, Estevan approached his friend Trenchant and asked:

"Can you land me on the coast of Cuba?"

"No; I would willingly do so if I could; but these men are so much in dread of the Spaniards that we dare not think of approaching Cuba. You must go with us to Florida; but you shall receive good treatment and be sent home as soon as possible."

"Going to Florida," thought Estevan. He was to be the guest of a Huguenot colony, a class of people whom he had been taught to hate. Surely Providence had laid a strange chain of circumstances to teach him humility.

The vessel steered directly for the river May in Florida, and Laudonnière, who had timely notice of the arrival of the pirate, appeared at the head of thirty well-armed soldiers and made all prisoners. None but La Croix and Stephens offered any resistance, and these were knocked down and secured before they could do mischief. Estevan, as well as the others, was put in irons and marched up to the fort, he and Trenchant being chained together.

On the way to the fort they heard the whining, hypocritical voice of Gyrot pleading with Laudonnière:

"Monsieur Laudonnière, good Monsieur Laudonnière, I was torn from your side, as you observed, and forced to become a pirate. It grieved my heart, monsieur, for I was very loyal to you, monsieur, oh I loved you well."

"Hear the hypocrite," hissed Trenchant. "He was the originator of the scheme, and now he seeks by the destruction of his accomplices to save his own neck—the traitor!"

The fort was reached and all were locked in dungeons for the night. Next morning Francisco Estevan was sent for by Laudonnière and hurried into the presence of the commandant.

"Trenchant has informed me that you are a Spaniard," said Laudonnière.

"I am, señor. I am a Cuban, born of Spanish parents."

"You were captured?"

"Yes, señor, while *en route* for Cuba from Spain."

"I regret very much that you have been subjected to this annoyance, and I can assure you that you are safe from further harm. I will send you to Cuba as soon as practicable; meanwhile you must remain our guest."

Estevan bowed and remained silent. Laudonnière had not said all he wished to say. After assuring the Spaniard that he was at liberty to come and go as he pleased, that he could answer or refuse to answer any questions, the commandant asked:

"Have they heard of this colony in Spain?"

"They have," Francisco answered.

"What do they say of it?"

"The king is very angry, and it is rumored he has commissioned Don Pedro Melendez to exterminate you."

Laudonnière was startled at this intelligence, and his face grew deathly white. After a few moments he said:

"I thank you for the information. We would truly be in a pitiable plight now to be attacked by Melendez. We seek only homes and peace, and right to exercise our religious liberty. Why should Philip II. refuse us this?"

With all his bigotry, early training, and superstition, Francisco Estevan was forced to admit the reason of the Huguenot's argument. He was silent, however, for he dared not trust himself to answer. After an awkward silence of several minutes, Laudonnière added:

"Whatever may be the result of this mad act of my unfortunate countrymen, you need fear no more harsh treatment at our hands."

"I wish to interpose a word for one of your countryman."

"Who?"

"Trenchant, the pilot. I have every reason to believe, from his treatment toward myself and all other prisoners, and his aversion to acting with his companions, that he was forced to become a pirate. He told me he was dragged on board, bound, and threatened with death."

"He shall be pardoned, while Gyrot, who seems to bear you a personal grudge, will be punished. I have sent for him and he is coming now."

"HE APPEARED MORE CUNNING AND FEROCIOUS IN IRONS THAN BEFORE."

At this moment the door opened, and Gyrot, escorted by two soldiers entered. He was more devilish, more cunning, and more ferocious in irons

than he had appeared before. In his suit of black
velvet, he looked not unlike a stage representation
of Richard III. A black cloak hung from his
shoulders, and on his wrists were handcuffs. His
pale face was surrounded by a mass of black hair
which fell almost to his slightly stooped shoulders.
Even with his wild eyes, the iris of which contracted or dilated at pleasure, his strongly devel-
oped facial angles, sharp nose, low forehead, livid
complexion, black hair and sharp white teeth, he
was politeness unexceptionable. He bowed to
Laudonnière and Estevan, and the horrible smile
which revealed those immaculate white teeth
played upon his face.

"What is monsieur's pleasure?" asked Gyrot,
with an effort to look pleasant and submissive.

"I have heard of your hatred of this Spaniard,"
answered Laudonnière.

"My hatred! Oh, monsieur, there is some mistake."

"There is not. Gyrot, you are a wolf in sheep's
clothing."

' Gyrot, assuming his meekest demeanor, bowed
and waited until the outburst of wrath on the part
of Laudonnière had somewhat subsided, and
answered:

"Many things monsieur says seem true, but if
he will listen, I can convince him I have been

greatly wronged. I know my life is forfeited; I am to die, and yet I don't complain. I only ask monsieur to let me clear up some of the charges against me."

"Proceed; make your defence," answered Laudonnière.

"The governor saw me overpowered by the mutineers and carried away. This gentleman, Francisco Estevan, will bear witness that I saved him when placed on the fatal plank and about to be pushed into the sea."

Laudonnière turned his eyes inquiringly upon Estevan.

"What he has said is true," Francisco answered, "But at the same time he said he reserved me for a greater punishment."

"Monsieur Commandant will understand I had to offer some such excuse to appease the pirates, and save his life."

So shrewdly did Gyrot conduct his own defence, so meek, so humble and penitent did he seem, that the commandant released him with only a rebuke, and ordered him, as he valued his life, to respect their Spanish guest. All the pirates did not fare so easily. Four of the most mutinous, including the Genevois, La Croix, and Des Fourneaux, were that day condemned to be hanged; but Laudonnière, at the earnest request of his men, changed the sentence to shooting, and an hour before sunset they were marched blindfolded to the spot where they were executed, and all were buried in one grave.

Finding himself unable to leave Florida at once, Francisco Estevan, in order to keep himself occupied, volunteered to join La Roche Ferriere in his successful tours of discovery. La Roche Ferriere had visited the Indians near the Appalachian Mountains, and had made alliances which excited the jealousy of Outina. He returned to Laudonnière with fine presents from the new friends of the French, consisting of gold and silver plate, curious quivers, furs, arrows ornamented with gold, hangings made of beautiful feathers, hatchets and other utensils.

On the first expedition in which Francisco Estevan accompanied La Roche Ferriere they learned that a chief, Onathaca, had in his possession two white men who were slaves, and who, upon promise of their ransom, would be sent to Carolinia.

"They must be two of my nationality," said Estevan to Laudonnière, who ordered the ransom paid and the prisoners to be brought to the fort. As Estevan had predicted, they proved to be Spaniards who had long been in slavery, having been lost in one of the exploring expeditions of the Spaniards. One of them had a piece of gold worth twenty-five crowns. Laudonnière, eager to learn all he could of the country, asked the oldest of the Spaniards to tell him all he knew of Florida. Through Francisco Estevan as interpreter the Spaniard said:

"Onathaca reigns over the eastern part of Florida; but toward the west reigns another king called Callos, who was owner of all the gold and silver mines of Florida. A great number of European vessels have been wrecked on his coast, which is quite dangerous for shipping. This prince has a ditch six feet deep and three wide filled with gold and silver ornaments. In his town are four or five European women of rank with their children who were wrecked on his inhospitable coast about fifteen years ago. This chief or king has great power over his subjects, who believe him to be a supernatural being. He has persuaded them that the fertility of the earth is owing to him, for which reason they sacrifice to him every year about harvest time an unhappy captive. I advise you not to trust the Floridians; they are treacherous dogs, and are most dangerous when making their greatest pretentions to friendship."

"How many men would it take to conquer Callos?" asked Laudonnière.

"With one hundred men we could put you in possession of Callos and also make other great discoveries."

Laudonnière merely said he would give the matter his attention and dismissed the Spaniards, assuring them that they could make their home in his colony. Instead of espousing the cause of any tribe of Indians, Laudonnière sought to reconcile them to each other, and formed alliances with many of their chiefs to which he intended to have recourse in case of new disturbances in his colony, or if the rumored invasion from Spain should prove to be a reality. He gave employment to his people by storing his magazines, and dispatched Ottigny, who took Francisco Estevan with him, on new discoveries. On this expedition they visited a great lake, the sand along the shore of which was thought to contain fine grains of gold. On their return to the fort they visited Outina, with whom, at his earnest request, Ottigny left some of his companions under Francisco Estevan.

Outina, finding himself involved in a fresh war with the son of Potanou, desired of Laudonnière a small force of men and guns, and Ottigny was sent to him with thirty auxiliaries. After a two day's march, Outina was a little dismayed to learn that his enemies were prepared to receive him, and his war juggler advised him to retreat, for young Potanou was waiting with two thousand warriors.

Outina was alarmed and on the point of turning

back, when Ottigny and Francisco called him a coward and pressed on with thirty soldiers armed with matchlocks. The onset began by a volley of musketry, which made such havoc among the enemy that the Indians fled in dismay, leaving Outina and his French allies master of the field.

On their return from this successful campaign, John Gyrot, who had hitherto kept aloof from Francisco Estevan, approached the Spaniard, and, in a voice full of irony, said:

"Monsieur makes a brave soldier; I congratulate him; but what has become of his priestly intentions?"

Turning a look of withering scorn on this human reptile, Francisco replied:

"Beware how you taunt me—you cur!"

CHAPTER VII.

THE more Francisco knew of Laudonnière,·the better he liked him. His kindness, genteel manner, and nobility of character recommended him to any fair-minded person. The noble commandant guaranteed him life and liberty while in the colony, and promised to send him and the other Spaniards to Cuba as soon as practicable. All knew it would be certain destruction for a French vessel to venture near the Cuban coast after the recent outrages of D'Oranger and his cut-throats. Laudonnière was found in very low spirits on their return from the campaign against Potanou.

"Monsieur, it is a desponding colony you see," Laudonnière said. "Truly we are all on the verge of despair."

"Why?" asked Estevan.

"Reinforcements and provisions, which Ribault was to bring from France, have not arrived, and our colony is again on the point of mutiny."

"The soil yields bountifully and would produce

all the provisions needful for the men. Why do not the colonists till more ground and devote more attention to their comforts than to exploring a wilderness in which Narvaez and De Soto lost their lives?"

"Alas, monsieur, there is the root of our calamity. Our people are unfitted to till the soil; they are not the hardy, industrious men of which pioneers are made. There are too many gentlemen and not enough laborers and farmers among them. We have too many consumers and too few producers."

Estevan thoughtfully answered:

"The same curse has fallen on every colony planted in the New World. It is not gentry but men of toil who are most needed here. As soon as the gold in the Spanish colonies is exhausted the soldiers and gentlemen will be forced to leave them. The mines at San Domingo are failing, and in a few years more will be completely exhausted."

At this moment D'Erlac entered the commandant's apartment.

"Monsieur D'Erlac, what news do you bring?" asked Laudonnière.

"The barbarians who have been charging us such exorbitant prices for food now refuse to sell at any price."

This was quite a shock to the commandant.

8

For several moments he was silent, and then, with a troubled brow, said:

"The heathen have abated their passion for trinkets, and, seeing our deplorable condition, are determined to take advantage of it. Have you been to see Outina?"

"Yes."

"How is he?"

"He says he has no more provisions to spare. That his wars have cost him dearly and his people have not had time to plant and grow corn."

"That is a sample of savage generosity," said Laudonnière. "Only a few weeks ago we sent armed men to help Outina defeat Potanou the younger; now he has turned his back upon us."

He was moved to tears by their deplorable condition, although he endeavored to encourage his people.

"Ribault will surely come soon," he declared. "Have patience; there is game in the forests and fishes in the streams."

He roused the desponding Frenchmen into something like activity, and they began to hunt and fish; but, as if by some evil power, the fish had disappeared from the streams and the game from the forests. Estevan, who was an experienced hunter, killed a fat buck, and the colony almost mutinied over the venison.

To add to their distress, the savages became bolder as the French grew weaker, and subjected them to divers insults which under no other circumstances would have been borne for a single instant.

The despairing men begged to return to France; but the thought seemed sheer madness. Their vessels were in no condition to weather the storms and currents of an Atlantic voyage; besides, they had neither sufficient food to last, nor the means of procuring enough for victualling the vessels.

They were compelled to subsist on acorns, herbs and roots, such as they could dig in the fields and forests. The Indians grew bolder in their insults every day, until at last they were so outrageous that Laudonnière ordered their town to be burned; but he repented of the order and recalled it almost immediately. The same evening Trenchant entered the cabin of Laudonnière with a serious look on his face and said:

"Monsieur, a savage has killed one of our men."

"Now I will burn their town!" cried Laudonnière, greatly angered, and at the head of a small party he went himself and set fire to the miserable huts where the Indians lived. The savages fled to the woods where they were secure, and the French returned not half satisfied with what they had done.

Day by day affairs grew worse. Estevan soon
felt the pangs of hunger. He was a good hunter,
was industrious, and alone he could have sup-
ported himself despite the dangers in the forests;
but there were so many too feeble to hunt, pluck
fruit, or dig roots that he was forced to yield a
greater share of his hard-earned food to them.
Yams, which grew in abundance in the forest, were
excellent food when baked, and in addition there
were oranges and other wild fruits.

On his return from a day of toil and peril in the
forest, he saw quite a commotion at the commandant's house, and drawing nearer he ascertained that
Gyrot, Trenchant, and others were pressing Laudonnière to arrest Outina and force him to furnish
them with the means of subsistence. Laudonnière
held out for a long time, but disease and famine
had made such inroads on his colony and so weakened his resolution, that at last he yielded. When
asked what he thought of the plan, Francisco
denounced it.

"It is unwise, and the act will only bring upon
us a disastrous war," he declared.

"He is a Spaniard and an enemy to the Huguenots," cried that mischief-maker of the colony,
John Gyrot.

"Spaniard though I be, our interests are one,"
Estevan proudly answered. "I am not your

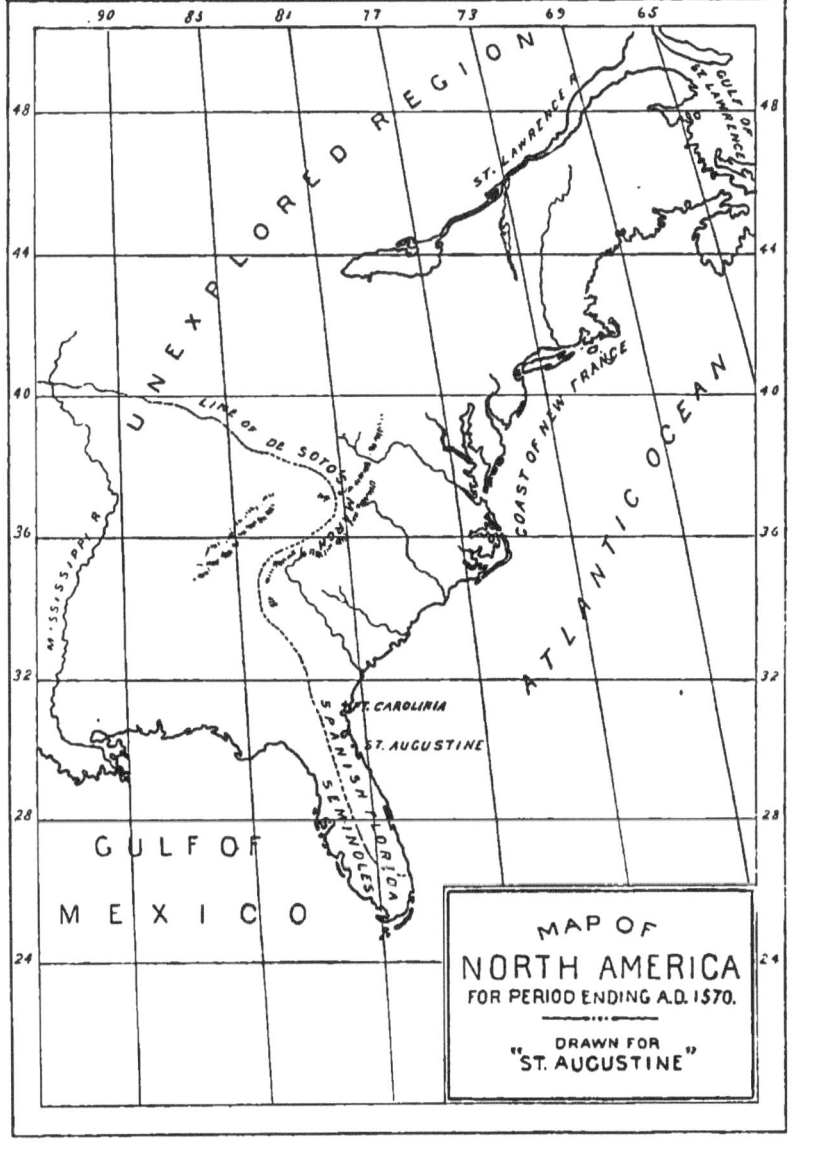

MAP OF
NORTH AMERICA
FOR PERIOD ENDING A.D. 1570.

DRAWN FOR
"ST. AUGUSTINE"

enemy. Our interests are mutual and your safety is mine."

But as drowning men grasp at a straw, the foolish Huguenots believed that with Outina a prisoner his people would furnish them with abundance of food, and all were eager for the arrest of the Indian chief.

"Why longer delay?" asked Gyrot. "We have the commandant's assent: what more do you want?"

"Nothing."

"Then to Outina let us go."

Twenty armed men set out for the distant village of Outina, and at midnight rushed into the hamlet while the people were buried in sleep, seized the chief, and dragged him from his bed. The rudely awakened savages uttered loud cries and fled to the wood, while Outina was carried to Fort Carolinia. Next morning after the return of the expedition with the captive, the savages, who had had time to recover their courage, were seen like a vast cloud hovering about the fort. D'Erlac, Estevan, and Trenchant were sent to negotiate with them.

"What do you want?" D'Erlac asked.

"Our chief," was the answer.

"And we want food," said the Frenchman. "Bring us food and we will restore Outina to you."

Some of the head men conferred a few moments, and one answered:

"We have no more food than we want for ourselves. The Frenchmen are idle vagabonds, and we do not care to support them. Why do they not plant and till the soil as we do, and not depend on us for subsistence?"

This was a truth which the embassadors could not deny. Their efforts to conciliate the Indians and secure food were unavailing.

"We want our chief," they declared; "and we will have him or make war on the white people until they are exterminated."

The envoys, finding their efforts at negotiation of no avail, returned to the fort and reported the result. The Indians hovered in a vast body on the north end of the wood, but a shot from one of the lombards dispersed them. They concealed themselves in the woods and assailed every Frenchman with arrows as soon as he ventured from the fort, so that the French dared not venture into the wood for game or roots. One man was killed and several wounded by the besieging foe. Being unable to hunt, fish, or dig roots, their condition became more desperate than it had been before. For three days they were virtually penned up in. their fort in a state of siege with starvation for the

chief guns. At the close of the third day Laudonnière declared:

"I am going to negotiate with the Indians and
release Outina on some terms."

Next morning he chose D'Erlac, Ottigny, and
Francisco Estevan as the bravest and coolest
advisers, and sent word to the Indians that he was
coming to treat with them. On his wishes becoming known a deputation of head men were sent to
meet the four white men.

"We don't wish to harm your chief; but we are
starving and must have food," said Laudonnière.

"We have no more food than we want ourselves,"
the Indians answered.

"Our ships will soon come from across the sea
and bring us relief."

This story was no longer credited by the Indians. They were not wholly unwilling to treat,
however, and agreed to give five measures of corn,
and a small quantity of yams and fruit, for the
restoration of their chief. For this trifle Laudonnière agreed to release Outina, and as the Indians
had the amount of ransom with them, he sent
Estevan to bring the chief under a guard of ten
soldiers, while the Indians got together the ransom.

"Beware!" whispered D'Erlac, "or they will
yet take some advantage of us."

The provisions were brought, and shortly after Estevan with ten soldiers brought the captive chief. The prisoner was freed, and with their limited amount of provisions the French started to the fort. They had gone but a short distance when a noise caused Estevan to glance behind him. "They are coming—beware!" he cried.

With yells the savages seemed to start up from the earth on every side. The soldiers had not time to set their matchlocks before the racks were overturned and they were engaged in a hand-to-hand encounter. Laudonnière was weak from sickness and lack of food, and though he drew his sword and fought like a lion, it became evident that he was unable to defend himself. Estevan, seeing his feeble condition, cried to D'Erlac and Ottigny:

"Defend the señor; he is too weak to resist them."

With their swords, the three beat back the savages and bore the commandant in safety to the fort.

The Indians retook all the provisions given in exchange for their chief, and two of the French soldiers were killed in the conflict.

The condition of the Huguenots was now deplorable. Some were too weak from sickness and famine to rise from the ground, and Francisco frequently found a feeble companion at night a

corpse in the morning. No more communication
was had with the Indians.

They determined to return to their native country, and work was begun on their vessels, when a
ship from France with a cargo of millet, came
into port. With a supply of nourishing food
the sick began to recover and the feeble grew
bolder; yet nothing could deter them from their
design of returning to France.

"What will monsieur do?" asked Laudonnière
of Francisco.

"Can you send me to Cuba?" he asked.

"Impossible."

"Then I will go to France."

Though he had not abandoned his idea of the
priesthood and regarded the Huguenots as heretics
and emissaries of the devil, his heart began to
flutter at thought of again being in the same country with Hortense. Youth is a flower of which
love is the fruit, and happy is he who, after watching its silent growth, is permitted to gather and
call it his own. Useless indeed to lay plans which
threaten to trample the affections; for love knows
no barriers, falters at no difficulties, and laughs
at bolts and bars.

The Huguenots were busy again with their preparations, when Gyrot, who had ventured below
the fort, gave utterance to a shout of joy.

"Deliverance has come! Deliverance has come!" he cried. "Behold ships from France!"

Four vessels were seen in the offing, and, believing them to be ships sent to relieve the colonists, the greatest demonstrations of joy were made by the Frenchmen. Shouting, singing, dancing, laughing and crying like children, they ran down to the bay.

Francisco Estevan, who shared their joy, was foremost in the race. His eyes were stronger and judgment clearer than his excited companions, and, after giving the vessels a careful inspection, he said:

"Those are not French ships; they fly English colors."

This discovery checked the joy of the French, but only for a moment. They knew the English were friendly to them and would give them aid, so once more their shouts of welcome rose on the air.

The vessels fired a salute which was answered by the fort, and a boat was seen to put off from the largest of the fleet to the shore. Laudonnière, surrounded by his staff, D'Erlac, Francisco Estevan, Ottigny, and Trenchant, went down to meet the boat and learn who the visitors were. The boat touched the strand, and a young sailor landed and approached the ragged colonists,

SHOUTING, SINGING, DANCING, LAUGHING AND CRYING, THEY RAN DOWN
TO THE BAY.

"Sir John Hawkins from England is in your bay with his fleet," he said, tipping his hat, "and he wishes to land and pay Laudonnière a visit, if he will permit him."

"Inform Sir John Hawkins that I shall be happy to receive him, and such poor hospitality as I can afford will be freely accorded him."

The sailor returned and Sir John Hawkins landed. His object in touching at the colony was to procure a supply of fresh water. Laudonnière conducted him to his house, where he treated him to some wild fowls, which Estevan had trapped the day before, and he was almost as

SIR JOHN HAWKINS.

happy to meet the generous Englishman as if he had been a brother.

"We are in a most wretched, starving condition," Laudonnière explained. "We have three deadly enemies to contend with: savages, famine, and the Spaniards." Laudonnière then narrated all that had transpired since he had come to the colony, not even omitting the piratical expedition against the Spaniards. The generous Englishman was greatly moved, and furnished the Frenchman with bread and wine, which neither the commandant nor his people had tasted for six or seven months before.

On seeing the ships in the bay, the savages supposed the long talked-of reinforcements had arrived from France and became more friendly, bringing stores of provisions from all quarters. Sir John Hawkins furnished the colonists with everything they stood in need of, and offered to carry them to France; but they declined this kind offer. Laudonnière, however, purchased one of his ships and determined to set sail for France by the fifteenth of the month.

It was August 1, 1565, when Sir John Hawkins bade the French colonists adieu and, with the remaining three vessels, spread his sails for England.

Estevan appealed to him to be taken to Cuba, where his parents had so long expected him; but several things conspired against the plan. First, they were bound for England; second, the feeling between Great Britain and Spain was not the best, and, as Sir John Hawkins, like Sir Francis Drake, was a sort of free rover, privateer, or pirate, he had some hesitation about landing in Havana. Thus Estevan again found his fate, by many uncontrollable destinies, linked with the Huguenots.

Fate destined him to return to France. Once

more he would probably see the only being who had ever stirred the tender emotions of his soul. If it were fate, why resist? He worked with others loading the ships, and by the fourteenth of August all were ready, and on the next morning would surely weigh anchor for France.

That night Francisco Estevan, who had remained on shore, was alone in his hut, his mind busy with bitter thoughts, and his soul engaged in a terrible struggle. Superstition and bigotry on one side was arrayed against love and reason.

"I will go to France; I will see Hortense De Barre," he said, half aloud. "I will once more gaze into those soulful eyes which seem to read my doom. She is the only one of God's creatures that ever awoke my slumbering affections. Does God will it? Has Providence brought about this chain of unforeseen circumstances which link us to each other? If God had not designed it, why was I, alone of all my ship's crew, rescued, and by her? Why was she placed at Beaucarre to receive me? I verily believe that when I land in France I will find Hortense De Barre to meet me! Do the saints send her?"

Then his traditions and bigotry got the better of him, and he fiercely cried:

"No, no! she is an emissary of the devil sent to tempt me as St. Anthony was tempted. Holy

Virgin, help me this moment! The flesh is so
weak; God, send thy saints to give me strength.
It is the devil—the devil that tempts me—I won't
love her—out of my sight, thou picture—thou
matchless creation of the prince of darkness! I
will—I will be a priest!"

Overwhelmed by his emotions, the young Spaniard fell on his face and burst into tears. He was
still moaning and sobbing, when Laudonnière
entered.

"What is wrong with my friend, what is amiss,
monsieur?"

"Señor, I am most miserable of all men."

"Why, Monsieur Estevan, what makes you
miserable?" asked the kind-hearted Laudonnière.
"You wish to return to Cuba. Wait until we
reach France. It will be easy for you to go to Spain,
and sail home in one of your ships."

"It is not that, señor—it is not that. There is
a conflict raging within. My heart prompts me to
one thing, my conscience to another. Tell me,
señor, is conscience ever wrong?"

Laudonnière gave him a surprised look.

"Generally, no; particularly, yes," he answered.
"Your conscience always says, do right—your
judgment tells you what is right. Now, if judgment has been perverted, wrongly educated, controlled by false logic and traditions, it is wrong,

and misleads conscience. Conscience misled is dangerous. Men may kill for conscience' sake, believing they do God service."

So much was his argument like that which Hortense used, that Estevan started to his feet, rushed out into the night, and, kneeling under a great live oak, prayed:

"Thou great God, whom we all worship, teach me what is right! Must I become a priest, or must I abandon the holy calling?"

CHAPTER VIII.

THE morning of the 15th of August, 1565, dawned, and the ships were all ready to put to sea. Every man was on board. Provisions sufficient to last them on the voyage had been placed in the holds and anchors were weighed; but a contrary head wind beat them back into the harbor, and, again casting anchor, most of them returned to shore.

This contrary wind continued until the 28th of the month, when it became once more fair and Laudonnière determined to sail. Again every one was ordered aboard, and they were in the act of weighing anchor when D'Erlac cried:

"There are ships at anchor in the bay."

Every eye was turned in that direction, and, sure enough, ships could be seen in full view.

"Who are they?" asked Laudonnière.

"I fear they are Spanish vessels," said D'Erlac.

"Doubtless sent to punish us for the acts of the pirates whom we shot," said Laudonnière uneasily.

128

Turning to Francisco Estevan, he asked, "What do you think of those ships? Are they Spanish or Portuguese vessels?"

"I am not certain," Francisco anwered. "I see no colors; but from the make of the vessels, they seem to be Spanish caravels."

Laudonnière was in deadly fear of the Spanish. He sent out a boat to speak with them. To his great surprise and alarm the boat did not return, so he ordered all his men to disembark and shutting himself up in his fort, determined to stand upon his defence.

The day passed and night closed in. It was a night of great anxiety on the part of the colony. At early dawn Laudonnière perceived seven chaloupes, full of armed people, proceeding in profound silence up the river.

"There can be no question that they are enemies," said Laudonnière; "but in order to be quite sure, fire a matchlock to show them we are aware of their approach."

D'Erlac's gun was loaded and the match burning. He sent a bullet speeding through the air which struck the water a few rods short of the advance boat. Laudonnière, mounting the wall of the fort, waved his sword in the air and cried:

"Hold—advance no further or we will sink your boats with our cannon."

9

The people in the chaloupes, greatly surprised, rested on their oars, while one answered: "Why do you fire on us? We are from France. Our ships are under Ribault, and we are coming with recruits and supplies for the colony."

Ribault, who was himself in the advance boat, felt no little indignation at his reception, though Laudonnière assured him he thought them enemies coming to attack them.

"You have great cause to dread the Spaniards," Ribault answered leaping on shore.

"What do you mean, monsieur?" Laudonnière asked. "Your language implies a rebuke."

"The doings of this colony have reached the ears of the king," Ribault answered. "It is reported that instead of clearing forests, planting fields, building towns and working mines, you have been carrying on piratical expeditions in the West Indies."

"Have such reports reached France?"

"They have, and they have tended to ruin not only you, but myself, and our patron, the Admiral Coligni."

Laudonnière assured Ribault that the charges against him were unjust, and that he had been cruelly maligned by the enemies of Protestantism. He called Trenchant and Estevan to prove that he had been overpowered by the vagabonds and forced to sign the commission, and that he had subsequently caused the chief conspirators to be shot.

"The act has almost overthrown our hopes," said Ribault. "The Catholics use it against us. It is thought Catharine de Medici is ready to espouse the cause of the Catholics as warmly as she has the Protestants. The act of piracy has roused PHILIP II., and I was informed that he had sent Don Pedro Melendez to exterminate the colony."

Laudonnière turned pale and asked:

"Have you brought more colonists?"

"I have, and among them are many women and children who are helpless and dependent on our arms for protection against the Indians and Spaniards. They left their own country to escape persecution, and came here, perhaps, to fall a prey to Melendez."

Estevan, who had overheard the remarks of the Frenchman, could no longer refrain from defending his countrymen.

"Señor, do not charge the Spaniards with such barbarity. Their religious zeal may drive them to war; but they are Christians and not savages, they will not make war on women and children."

"I hope not," Ribault answered, with a sad shake of his head as if he still doubted. "There is on board one of our vessels a young girl who lost her parents and only brother in the persecutions of the Huguenots. Her father and brother were

killed in a riot and their mangled bodies dragged
through the streets before her gaze."

"Her name—her name—" interrupted Francisco.

"Hortense De Barre."

Francisco Estevan suppressed a cry, and, turning hastily, quitted the fort. He was not strong
enough to meet her now, and, like one bewildered,
he wandered on over hills and through woods until
he came to the village of Saturiova. He had
become a warm friend of this chief and was welcomed by him to his lodge. Francisco had learned
something of the Indian tongue and could converse very readily with the Indians.

"More white men have come in the big canoes?"
asked Saturiova.

"Yes; they come from France."

"And white men will not go away?"

"No."

Noticing that Estevan was in great trouble, he
sought to comfort him, but in vain. With sighs
and in silence the student passed the day in the
home of the Indian. Many prayers did he utter,
and many times did he bow before and kiss the
small crucifix which he carried with him; but no
relief came to his mind. Saturiova sent his
daughter, an amiable damsel of eighteen, to restore
the sunlight to the young white man's face; but

the Indian beauty had no charm for him. He retired to the wigwam set apart for him, and after a sleepless night rose early next morning, and, bidding the chief adieu, started to return to Fort Carolinia.

He had fortified himself with prayers and believed himself strong enough to meet her; but, alas, how often we overestimate our strength. As he neared Fort Carolinia, he found his heart wildly fluttering, and his cheek flushing with a burning crimson.

Some of the ships had been hauled close in and the emigrants debarked. Munitions of war and stores of provisions were being unloaded. Estevan slowly approached the fort, his heart still beating wildly. Pausing on the hilltop to gaze on the animated scene, he saw men, women, and children moving about within the stockade. Then he caught sight of a figure, which caused a strange thrill to pass through his already excited frame. A bit of animated sunlight dancing here and there, flitting about like a gold-winged butterfly. That strange old feeling so delightful, and at the same time so miserable, once more possessed him. What were penance and prayer, against such an irresistible avalanche of emotion?

With faltering step he advanced toward the fort, asking himself how she would greet him. For the time being the lover had supplanted the priest.

Entering the fort, he was greeted by strange

faces.   Little bright-eyed children were making the gloomy place ring with their merry prattle.   It seemed as if the birds which had been driven from the woods had again returned.   Where was Hortense?   He was quite sure he had seen her from the hilltop.   Had she fled at his approach?   As Estevan was going around one of the buildings, a voice suddenly greeted his ear which thrilled him anew.   He paused and listened to the words, and anger and disgust began to supplant every other feeling.   Hortense was saying:

"John Gyrot, had I known I should find you here, I would have remained in France.   Better to die a Christian martyr at the stake than suffer this indignity at your hands."

The soft, hypocritical voice of Gyrot, sounding like the purr of a tiger, answered:

"Mademoiselle is excited, she must recover her self-possession.   The voyage was too much for her."

"The voyage, tedious and uncomfortable as it was, was nothing compared to your hateful presence for a moment.   God forgive me—I loathe and despise you."

"Mademoiselle will need a protector in the wilderness and I will be her protector.   Here is a wilderness, a savage people, the rude frontiersmen, and the Spaniards, all to be guarded against.   Who, save the mademoiselle's devoted slave, should be here to protect her?"

"Protect me, indeed! Heaven deliver me from such protection!"

For the first time since Francisco's acquaintance with Gyrot, the Frenchman's temper got the better of him. Leaping at the defiant girl, he seized her hand.

"Hortense De Barre!" he hissed, his hot breath scorching her cheek. "You can't escape me. Fate has decreed that you be mine, and mine you shall be. Don't think that any part of the world can conceal you from me."

"Let me go!"

"Not until you hear me through."

"Wretch, release me!"

"You shall listen, mademoiselle——"

At this point Francisco Estevan became irresponsible for his own acts. Reason, judgment, bigotry, and tradition were all supplanted by a whirlwind of emotions. Before he was aware of what he was doing, he held the half-fainting Hortense in his arms, while at his feet lay John Gyrot, stunned and bleeding. Francisco found himself uttering some strange, wild words, half in Spanish and half in French. He hardly knew what he was saying, and when he had recovered his presence of mind sufficiently to remember anything, he could not recall a single word he had uttered.   He still clung to Hortense, as if fearing they would be separated.   He led her away from the fallen scoundrel to another part of the fortification, and, when beyond hearing of Gyrot's curses and threats, and sight of his ugly face, made more hideous by the blackened eye and bleeding nose, they sat down on a bench beneath an oak.

Up to this moment, Hortense had not spoken a word since her rescue.   Dread and amazement had paralyzed her powers of speech; but now with eyes wide open she gazed at him and gasped:

"Monsieur Estevan!"

"It is I, señorita," he answered.   "I, who left you so abruptly—so unkindly, after you had saved my life at the peril of your own.   Señorita, I was very ungrateful—will you forgive me?"

"I have nothing to forgive.   I am amazed to find you here."

"I can explain my presence."   Then he told her how he was captured by the French pirate and brought to Florida.   She listened with rapt attention to the thrilling narrative from beginning to end, and, at the conclusion, said:

"Terrible, indeed!   What sympathy need the Huguenots expect, when they set such a dreadful example?"

"Your best people are not to blame," replied

Francisco. "I saw the chief criminals punished with death for the part they had taken."

"What are you going to do now?" she asked.

"I know not," Francisco answered. "The return of Ribault with recruits and supplies has deranged all plans. It was my intention to go to France and from thence to Spain to take passage in the first ship bound for the West Indies."

They spent the day in each other's society and lived over again those happy days at Beaucarre, and, notwithstanding, the perils by which they were surrounded, Hortense was almost happy.

Next morning Estevan arose early and strolled out upon the green in front of the house which had been erected by himself. The morn was bright and clear, and one would scarcely dream that an awful night was destined to follow. Some Catholics had come in Ribault's ships, and Francisco was conversing with one of these on the future of the colony and the propagation of their faith in the New World, when an officer came up and arrested the young Spaniard.

"What have I done, that I should be arrested?" Francisco asked.

"You assaulted Monsieur Gyrot."

Francisco had scarce given the matter a moment's thought before. He quietly submitted to the arrest and a moment later was put in irons. His case was more serious than one might at first suppose. Those petty governors had control of the lives and liberties of their subjects. He was a Catholic and a Spaniard, both of which created strong prejudices against him in the Huguenot colony. His friend Laudonnière was himself under a cloud and would probably not be able to render him any aid, while he rightly supposed that the cunning John Gyrot had ingratiated himself into the good graces of Ribault.

As he was being led along the street, some one suddenly sprang before him, a voice uttered a cry of amazement, and, like the flash of a sunbeam, the pretty, agitated face of Hortense was gazing into his.

"Is monsieur a prisoner?" she asked.

"I am, señorita."

"For what offence?"

"Striking Gyrot while insulting you."

"Shame! shame!" cried the brave girl, her large, beautiful eyes swimming with tears.

"Stand aside, mademoiselle, stand aside," commanded the guard.

"Monsieur, they shall not convict you."

"If they do, I will have the approval of my conscience, and, whatever my punishment may be, I will bear it with pleasure for your sake."

When Francisco Estevan was arraigned before Ribault he was informed that he was charged with a murderous assault on Monsieur Gyrot.

"Oh, no, it was not murderous, monsieur governor," whined a hypocritical voice, and, turning his eyes in that direction, Estevan saw the broad, low forehead, angular features, long black hair and white teeth of Gyrot, his left eye badly blackened. He was near Ribault, rubbing his hands, while his face was wreathed with smiles of mock sympathy for the accused.

"What have you to say to the charge?" asked Ribault.

"I am guilty of no penal offence, señor. I was passing through the fort when I heard a cry for help—" began Francisco, when John Gyrot interrupted him with:

"Monsieur is the accused and cannot give testimony."

The trial had excited universal interest, and the large room designated as the governor's hall was densely packed with spectators. Gyrot's words had scarcely died away when a sweet, clear voice cried:

"I can testify; I was a witness to the assault."

It was Hortense, and a murmur went over the assembly as she crowded through. The impression made by John Gyrot was not favorable, and when it became known that the fair Huguenot was

coming to the relief of her rescuer, she was greeted
with a cheer.

A smile was on Gyrot's devilish face as he said:
"She is under age and cannot give evidence,
governor."

"You cannot be a witness, mademoiselle," said
Ribault. "I am sorry, but Monsieur Gyrot has the
law on his side."

Hortense burst into tears, and a scene followed
which beggars description. Gyrot, with his demoniacal face all aglow with triumph, proceeded to
give his evidence. He made out a clear case of un-
provoked assault. He bore up well under a strong
cross-examination, and at the conclusion of his
evidence a death-like silence fell over the court.

What sentence would Ribault give the young
Spaniard? The lightest that could be hoped for
would be banishment from the colony, which was
sure to result in death in the forest or slavery
among the Indians. Ribault bowed his face in his
hands like a man who has a disagreeable task to
perform—one from which he shrinks.

Suddenly a commotion was heard without, and
the voices of Laudonnière and D'Erlac could be
heard saying:

"We must see Ribault—we must see the governor."

Ribault, hearing their demand, ordered them to

be admitted at once. Laudonnière's face betrayed unusual excitement as he said:

"We have no time for petty trials for misdemeanors, governor; for the Spanish with six men-of-war are on our coast."

Cries of rage and groans of despair went up from the colonists at the announcement, and it required several moments for Ribault to restore order. Turning to Estevan he said:

"The execution of this case will be stayed; meanwhile the prisoner will have his liberty."

Ribault hurried from the hall. Donning armor and arms, he ran to his boat, and, with half a dozen oarsmen, rowed out to the French ships, which had cut their cables and stood in up the river to keep from being taken by the Spaniards. Only a part of the French fleet had put into the river, the remainder having stood out to sea. After a consultation with the officers of his ships, Ribault returned to the fort. The Spanish fleet could be seen manœuvering along the coast; but it was uncertain whether they intended entering the harbor or not.

"What are their intentions?" asked Laudonnière, who was first to greet the governor on his return.

"Extermination," was the answer. "They ran up within hailing distance of one of our vessels, and demanded to know their nationality.

"'France,' was the answer.

"'And what are you doing in the territory of King Philip?' he asked. 'Begone!' he added. Then a moment later asked: 'Are you Catholics or Lutherans?'

"'Lutherans of the new.religion,' answered our officer. 'Now, what is your errand to this part of the world?'

"The Spanish office replied:

"'I am Pedro Melendez, the commander of this armament, which belongs to the king of Spain, Don Philip II. I have come hither to hang or destroy all the Lutherans whom I shall find on land or sea, according to my orders received from my king, which are so precise as to deprive me of the power of saving any one whatsoever. These orders I shall execute to the letter; but if I should meet with any Catholic on board your vessels, he shall receive good treatment. As for the heretics they shall die.'"

At this terrible intelligence, a wail went up on the air from the women and children; while the men shuddered and clung to their arms.

Estevan stood a little apart from the others; while at his side was Hortense De Barre. She turned her white face toward him, and a silent tear stole down her cheek, as she asked:

"Monsieur, does your religion condemn me to die?"

This question—this affecting appeal was too much for the young Spaniard, and, seizing her in his arms, in a voice which trembled with earnestness and emotion, he answered:

"No! Hortense. Pope or no pope, devil or no devil, you shall be saved!"

CHAPTER IX.

THE land and sea shook with the report of a cannon. One of the Spanish ships was bearing down on one of the French vessels when the latter fired a gun at her. The shot was returned, and for a few moments the forests along the bay rang with heavy cannonading; then the Spanish fleet stood out a little into the road and dropped anchor, while all became quiet, and the French ships drew up closer under the fort.

Although Melendez touched at the Florida coast on the 28th of August, it was not until the 4th of September that he reached the May or St. Johns River. His arrival with his fleet threw the French into a terrible state of excitement. A flock of sheep hemmed in by a pack of ravenous wolves could not have been more excited than they at this moment. Ribault called a council of war, from which Estevan, being a Spaniard and Catholic, was of course excluded. The council was held in the large hall in which Estevan had been tried.

144

"The situation is grave," said Ribault, "yet we are Frenchmen, and Frenchmen are not cowards. Let us seriously deliberate on the best plan for attacking the enemy."

Laudonnière, being asked his opinion, stated:

"The best we can do is to complete the works on Fort Carolinia in order to protect the women and children of the colony. Then, as the Spanish vessels can not come near enough to attack us, their forces must of necessity land on the coast. Let us send a strong detachment of troops by land to fall upon them while disembarking."

At this point of the conference, Ribault produced a letter from Coligni, advising him of the expedition of Melendez and enjoining him to suffer the Spaniards to do nothing prejudicial to the crown of France in Florida, and gave his opinion for attacking the Spaniards by sea. Nearly all the council opposed this resolution.

"It will not do, monsieur," said Laudonnière. "The season of hurricanes is approaching, and should your fleet be caught in one of these, you would be scattered and in all probability wrecked."

"Yet most of us are sailors," said Ribault. "We equal the Spaniards in guns and courage. We can suddenly fall upon their ships and sink them."

The commander of the French fleet, Cossel, and Ribault's son, who was master of one of the vessels,

10

sided with Ribault in his proposition to attack by sea.

"It is dangerous," persisted Laudonnière, "It will prove fatal to all our plans and may result in the destruction of our colony. If our forces are divided they will fall upon us and defeat us."

"Our forces will not be divided," said the determined Ribault. "I will take them all to sea, leaving only a sufficient number in the fort to defend the women and children."

Estevan, who lingered near the door, heard this stubborn determination of the governor of the colony, and his heart sank within him. He went hurriedly to find Hortense, whom he discovered waiting near the gate, pale and trembling.

"Hortense, will you promise to be very brave?" he said.

"What do you mean, monsieur?" she asked.

"Will you trust me to save you?"

She looked at him a moment, her great blue eyes seeming to read his heart, and then she answered: "I will."

"I swear by all the saints I will save you; but you must trust wholly in me."

"I trust alone in you and God."

"The danger is greater than these people imagine. Ribault is mad. He intends to attack the Spanish by sea, and his forces will be divided.

Even if he takes their ships he will lose his fort."

"God have mercy on us."

"But trust me, Hortense, I will save you. Say nothing to any one of this promise."

"Will the Spaniards be so cruel as to slay all?"

"Melendez declares that they will. They are more devils than Christians. But night is falling and I must go. Whatever may happen, I will return in time to save you."

They were alone, and, overcome by his overwhelming emotion, the young Spaniard clasped her a moment in his arms and whispered:

"No father, no brother, no lover was ever more watchful over the object of his adoration than I shall be."

He was gone, and the shades of evening were creeping over the fort. Long she stood wondering where he would go and what his plan for her safety would be. A step near at last startled her, and, on looking up, she saw John Gyrot, who had just come from the council hall.

"Mademoiselle," said Gyrot, with a hypocritical attempt to appear very much unconcerned, "Ribault has decided to attack by sea. If he does so, the Spaniards may assault by land. Will not mademoiselle place herself under my protecting care?"

"No;" and she turned away.

"Mademoiselle does not appreciate the danger. It is great.   Trust me and live."

"Away!   I hate you.   Death and Spaniards are preferable!"

Gyrot recoiled before her withering scorn, and slunk away from the fort, disappearing in the darkness.   He had heard that Melendez would give good treatment to any of the Catholics.   The promise made a strong impression on him, and, with that wonderful foresight which some men possess, he read the doom of the French.   He decided to go to Melendez that very night and secretly play the spy upon his people.   He knew enough of the language for his purpose.

At midnight a form stole through the wood to the path leading to a small Indian hamlet near the sea-coast.   The person was John Gyrot.   Reaching the Indian village, he went to one of the miserable lodges and roused an inmate with whom he conversed for a few moments in the Indian tongue. The subject of their discussion was evidently a very grave matter, for Gyrot was much in earnest. At last the Indian yielded to his bribes and the two stole away toward the coast two miles distant, where lay a large canoe among some tall rushes in the mouth of a creek.   They launched the boat, and, getting into it, paddled toward the Spanish fleet, which had not yet weighed anchor, directing the prow of their craft toward Melendez's flag ship. When a short distance away they were discovered and hailed by the guard on deck.

Gyrot answered in Spanish—boldly declaring himself a friend come to see Melendez. Melendez was notified of the request and ordered both to be brought on board.

"Well, señor, what is the object of this visit?" asked the admiral.

Gyrot bowed low, and, softly squeezing the palms of his hands together, said:

"Knowing the object of the admiral's visit to Florida, and, being a good Catholic, I came to give what information you may desire about Fort Carolinia."

"Are you a Frenchman?"

"Yes, monsieur; but a good Catholic."

"You came from the Huguenot fort?"

"Yes, monsieur; but I am a good Catholic, believing in the transubstantiation of the elements of the bread and wine at the consecration of the Lord's Supper into the real body and blood of Christ. I believe in the invocation and adoration of the Virgin Mary and all the saints, as well as the sacrifice of the mass as now used by the Church at Rome; and I believe in the infallibility of the Pope."

Melendez was taken by surprise at the unexpected

visit and declaration. After Gyrot had finished, he asked:

"Why did you come aboard my ship?"

"I learned your object was to exterminate the heretics. I overheard the plans of Ribault for resisting and attacking the Catholics, and came to inform monsieur that he might take advantage accordingly." Then Gyrot, whom Melendez thought a worthy disciple of Judas Iscariot, proceeded to relate the plans of Ribault for attacking him at sea, leaving only a slender garrison on land. When the Spaniard had heard Ribault's plan, he ordered anchor hoisted and the fleet was got under way.

The departure of the Spaniards was witnessed by Cossel, who at once reported to Ribault, which more than ever determined the commandant to attack by sea. Ribault was a sailor and accustomed to making the deck of his ship his battle-field, and he deserves not the censure for his mode of attack accorded him by some historians.

He mustered his men, and at roll-call John Gyrot was missing. Where was he? No one knew, and certainly no one guessed that he was at that very moment on board the ship of Melendez.

Laudonnière was left in the fort with but fifty men to protect the women and children; but Laudonnière was himself sick and not above twenty of his command were fit for active service. While Ribault was making preparations to attack Melen· dez by sea, an Indian came with the intelligence that the Spaniards had landed at a river several miles south of Fort Carolinia, and were laying out a town and building a fort for their defence.

This Indian was the savage who had accompanied Gyrot, and he had been sent to play the part of a spy on the Frenchmen.

Ribault hastened all his force, save the small garrison left to defend the fort, on board the ships. The *Trinity*, his largest vessel, was yet at sea, having been chased out by the approach of the Spaniards, who were unable to take her. Mendoza, the Spanish chaplain, said of the officers and sailors of this ship:

"These enraged devils are such adroit seamen, and manœuvered so well, that we could not take one of them."

The fiery Ribault, disregarding the advice of a majority of his councillors, sailed out of the river and down the straight coast in full expectation of gaining a complete victory. They came in sight of the Spaniards in the river about the middle of the afternoon and began to tack against an unfavorable breeze to get at them; but a dead calm following the discovery, aided by a low tide, made it impossible to reach them. The sun went down behind the swamps and forests leaving them within two miles of the enemy.

"We shall have wind and tide to aid us in the morning," said Ribault to his officers, "and then we will teach the king of Spain a lesson."

Had wind and tide favored him, Ribault might have made good his boast; but, alas, as every sailor on the southern coast of the United States knows, the dead calm too often precedes a storm. Ribault, having made everything snug on his vessel, had retired to his cabin to snatch a little sleep, and had just sunk into a gentle slumber, when Cossel awoke him, saying:

"It has begun to blow, monsieur. Hadn't we better stand off the shore?"

"Yes." Ribault rose and dressed hurriedly.

By the time he had gained the deck the wind was roaring like so many demons through the rigging of the vessel; while the waves were bounding like race-horses in their wake.

"Can we hold the fleet together?" Ribault asked Cossel, whom he found on deck issuing orders with remarkable coolness.

"I fear not," the sailor answered.

"Who is at the helm?"

"Trenchant. He is the most experienced pilot we have."

"It blows hard, Cossel,"

"It does, monsieur; but I hope it will not last long."

"I wish it would clear; but I doubt it much. I was once in a hurricane in the East Indies, and the beginning had much the same appearance as this. So take in your topsails and give yourself plenty of sea-room."

At midnight the storm was still raging they wore ship to keep away from the dangerous shoals and reefs. At one o'clock in the morning the gale was still increasing. At two it blew harder. They reefed the courses and furled them, and stood to the northward.

Ribault gazed out at the sea lashed to foam, hoping every friendly blaze of lightning might give him a glimpse of the other vessels. At last, as the sky and sea were lighted by one of these streaks of liquid flame, he saw far to their larboard a single sail. Was that all of the gallant fleet which, a few hours before, he had arrayed against the Spaniards? Three of the smaller ships, on board one of which was Ribault's son, hugged the shore until morning, and entered the river below Fort Carolinia.

There was nothing for Ribault to do but prepare, as best he could, to weather the storm. All the sails were secured with spare gaskets, good rolling tackle upon the yards, the booms were

squared and all the bolts made fast, the guns
doubly lashed and, in fact, everything possible was
done to make the ship snug.

At dawn of day the hurricane was roaring, and
the sea so rough it seemed as if the vessel must
founder. The birds now began to find the uproar
in the elements too much for them; for numbers,
both sea and land kinds, came on board the struggling, groaning ship. When they dropped upon
the deck, exhausted from their efforts to fly against
the wind, they did not attempt to stir until picked
up, and when let go they would not leave the ship,
but endeavored to hide themselves from the wind.

"It blows a hurricane, Cossel," said Ribault.

"It does indeed, monsieur."

"I don't remember ever seeing it blow so hard
before. We must wear ship a little as the wind has
shifted, and we are drawing right down upon the
coast."

It was difficult to change the course of the vessel in such a storm; but, after considerable danger
and the loss of one man, they succeeded, though the
ship did not make as good weather on this as on
the other tack; for the sea began to run across her,
and she had not time to rise before another dashed
against her.

All day long the tempest raged, and with the
coming of night it seemed to increase.

Even Ribault was almost in despair. He saw the easy victory snatched from his grasp by the fury of the hurricane, and now his fleet was scattered—where, he knew not. With his pale, stoical face turned toward the terrific blast, he stood in the extreme forward part of his ship, rising and sinking with the motion of the vessel. Could it be that fate had set the seal of doom against him?

"Monsieur, the vessel is leaking," said Cossel.

"Man the pumps!"

"The pumps are already at work."

Another ugly sea, and the water was gaining on them rapidly. They had broken one of the chains; but it was soon mended. A sailor was sent to report how deep the water was in the hold.

"It still gains on us," he answered on returning. "There is back water from the leeward half-way up the quarter-deck, the ship is on her beam ends, and is not attempting to right again, so the men cannot stand at the pumps."

The vessel evidently was doomed. Some one suggested cutting away the masts as the only possible means of saving the craft; but at this moment a violent sea broke right on board, carrying away everything on deck and filling the hold with water. The main and mizzen masts went, and the ship righted; but it was the last struggle; she was sinking. As soon as Ribault could shake his

head clear he saw the gallant Cossel still on deck
and Trenchant at the helm, which he had never
deserted, and he said:

"Noble fellows, it is all in vain! we are gone—
foundered at sea!"

"Yes, monsieur, farewell, and may the Lord
have mercy on our souls."

Ribault then turned to look about the ship and
saw that she was struggling to get rid of some of
the water; but it was all in vain—she was almost full below.   He began to pray:

"Almighty God! I thank Thee that now I am
leaving this world which I have always considerd
as only a passage to the better.   I die with the
full hope of Thy mercies, through the merits of
Jesus Christ Thy Son, our Saviour!"

Ribault regretted that he could swim, as it was
only natural for a man to struggle for his life as
long as he could, and the act of swimming would
probably prolong his misery.

These sad reflections were put to an end by a
sudden thump of the vessel and the sound of her
keel grinding on the sand.

"Monsieur, the ship is ashore and we may save
ourselves yet," cried Cossel.

The roar of the waves could be heard upon the
sandy beach, and the phosphorescent, flashing
spray, like flames leaping from hell, burst on their

startled view. By this time the quarter-deck was full of men flying up from below crying:

"Lord God, have mercy on us!"

Everybody was sensible of the fact that the ship was on shore, for every surging billow threatened her destruction. She was driven stern into the sand, the bow breaking the sea to a considerable extent, though it was washing clear over at every surge. Ribault, who was still cool, seeing their peril cried:

"Keep to the quarter-deck; when she goes to pieces it is your best chance."

Day dawned at last and the rising sun fell on a large group of dripping castaways gazing on the fragments of wreck strewn along the beach. They were Ribault and his brave seamen.

CHAPTER X.

MELENDEZ or Menendez (as the name is sometimes spelled) was a native of Avila in Spain, and
at this period of our story was about forty-six

MELENDEZ.

years of age. He had al-
ready risen to the highest
rank in the Spanish navy
and was a man of immense
fortune. He commanded
the vessel which in 1554
bore his king to England
to marry Queen Mary; and
in 1561, he commanded the
great treasure fleet of gal-
leons on their voyage from
Mexico to Spain. One of the vessels, containing
his son and several relatives and friends, disappeared and was never heard from. Having delivered the fleet in Spain, he asked permission to
go in search of the lost vessel and his son, but
was refused. After repeated solicitations, however,

when two or three years had elapsed, his urgent request was granted, provided he should at the same time explore and colonize Florida. He fitted out an expedition at his own expense; but when he was about to sail, orders came for him to exterminate all Protestants he might find there, or in whatever corner of the earth he should discover them.

King Philip learned that the Huguenots, flying from the persecutions in France, were hiding in the forests beyond the Atlantic, and his zeal being kindled for the denomination of his church, he determined to destroy the heretics in this way. The sailor had no alternative but to obey or lose the opportunity of searching for his son. It is said by some historians, who seek to throw a mantle of charity over the actions of Melendez, that not even this alternative was left him; for disobedience in that rigorous age would have led to dungeons and the Inquisition. We are led to believe, however, that Melendez entered as heartily into the bloody work as did his king. Regarding it as a holy enterprise, the king added ships and treasure. Soldiers and seamen flocked to the standard of Melendez in great numbers, and he sailed with a fleet of eleven ships (one of them a galleon of nine hundred tons) with over twenty-six hundred persons, consisting, besides soldiers and sailors, of adventurers and priests.

This was the armament of the sailing of which Ribault had been warned by Coligni. Storms and disasters scattered the fleet so that when it arrived on the coast of Florida, it was reduced to a squadron of only five vessels, one of them (the great ship) bearing about a thousand persons of all descriptions.

His first landing on the coast of Florida, after leaving May River, was the occasion of a pompous ceremonial. As he disembarked from the great ship in a boat with six oarsmen, accompanied by Mendoza, his chaplain, and followed by other boats, filled with gentlemen and ecclesiastics, loud trumpets sounded, drums beat, cannon thundered, and flags were displayed on the ships and on the shore, where his soldiers had already begun the construction of a fort.

John Gyrot, who was playing the part of a zealous Catholic, and who, by his cunning and address, had already ingratiated himself into the favor of the Spanish admiral, was permitted to accompany him to the shore and take part in the pompous ceremonial.

When they reached the beach, the chaplain walked before, bearing a large cross and chanting a hymn. Melendez followed with his own train, carrying aloft with his own hand the royal standard. He and his followers reverently knelt before the priest, who was arrayed in rich sacerdotal robes, and kissed the sacred emblem of the atonement, which Mendoza held in his hand. Then the cross was firmly planted in the sand by the side of the flagstaff, from which fluttered the royal banners in the gentle breeze, and a shield bearing the arms of Spain was leaned against the cross. Then Melendez drew his sword and formally took possession of the whole country in the name of King Philip of Spain. The Spanish conquerors never lacked in religious zeal and pompous ceremony. From Columbus down to Melendez, every conquest of nation or territory was begun with a gorgeous religious ceremony.

On that spot, and with such consecration, were laid the foundations of the city of St. Augustine, in Florida, forty years earlier than any other town in America north of Mexico. This town, small and insignificant as it is from a business point of view, possesses the distinction of being the oldest in the United States. It was named St. Augustine after the river Dauphin, which Melendez gave the name of St. Augustine, because he discovered it on that saint's day, prior to reconnoitering the French fort Carolinia.

Work was at once commenced on the fort, and the Spaniards, fully appreciating the necessity of having a place of security, labored with unremit-

11

ting zeal. Gyrot still remained with the Spaniards;
but the Indian had wandered off, and gone to Fort
Carolinia to report what the Spaniards were doing,
as we have seen.

"I should like to talk with monsieur," said
Gyrot to Melendez the day work was commenced
on the fort.

"What would señor say?" asked Melendez.

"Had I not better return to Carolinia?   May not
my absence rouse suspicion?"

Melendez was not sure he could trust Gyrot, and
he asked:

"Do you intend to betray us?"

"No, monsieur.   I only want to return to soothe
the fears of my people by assuring them that the
Spaniards have abandoned the coast."

"I don't believe I can trust you."

"I swear, monsieur, by all the saints that I am
loyal to you.   Will you not take the oath of a
true Catholic, who believes in the transubstantiation
of the bread and wine into the real body and blood
of Christ, who prays to the Virgin Mary and the
saints, and is a believer in the sacrifices of mass as
practised at Rome, who knows the Pope to be
infallible?   On the holy cross, I swear to be true
and loyal to Melendez."

In the age of superstition and bigotry, perjury,
it was thought, would be visited by immediate

punishment at the hand of God. Deliberate, bold perjury was not so common as it is in the present age of skepticism.

Melendez, if he lived at this day, would put little faith in the pretensions and oaths of Gyrot; but the Melendez of 1565 was quite a different personage.

Upon the cross Gyrot swore to be faithful to the Spaniards and to do whatsoever he could to bring confusion and disaster on the heretics. In return he asked Melendez that a certain maiden, Hortense De Barre, should be given to him. Finally the Spanish commandant agreed to all he asked. After these solemn promises and the awful compact to be sealed in the innocent blood of his countrymen, John Gyrot took his departure on the evening of the 9th of September, 1565, and set out across the country for Fort Carolinia, his mind busy with cunning schemes for bringing disaster upon the French.

Work was progressing on the fort next day, the 10th of September, when the vessels of Ribault hove in sight. Though his works were far from complete, Melendez retired within them, determined to stand on his defence. The tide was out and there was a dead calm; so they had little to fear before morning. Ribault was a desperate seaman and one well calculated to inspire dread in the hearts of the Spaniards. Mendoza performed mass, and officers and soldiers prayed for aid from Heaven in defeating the enemies of the Holy Catholic church.

To them it always seemed as if God answered their prayers; for, as we have seen, a terrible hurricane rose, and the French fleet was driven away and hopelessly scattered. When morning came, Melendez summoned all his officers and a great many of his soldiers about him. Although some of their own shipping had suffered by the storm, he treated it as a providential interference in their behalf.

"See how good God is to us," he said. "Our enemies surrounded us; we were weaker than they; but God sent the hurricane which scattered them. The hurricane was a divine judgment upon the heretics, and who shall say that we will fail, when God fights our battles? So long as we do His holy will we shall triumph, and it is His wish that we destroy all who deny the faith and despise the Pope. It is the will of God that we attack Fort Carolinia by land. The good Catholic whom Heaven sent us has told us how weak is the fort. Laudonnière is there with not over forty men, while Ribault, with all the others, has been driven to sea. Let us, the instruments of God's vengeance, fall upon and exterminate the heretics."

Notwithstanding the religious zeal and enthusiasm of Melendez, there was at first some opposition to his plan. Laudonnière, the old battle-scarred veteran, was there, and, sick and weak as he might be, he was a host in himself; but Melendez assured them that he had from Gyrot positive proof that Laudonnière was two feeble to make much resistance.

After a warm debate, the counsel at last consented to the attack. The hurricane had been accompanied by a tremendous rain-storm, and the low lands were in many places overflowed, while sluggish streams were swollen until they were out of their banks.

With his heart fired with bigoted zeal, and in the insane belief that he was doing the will of God, Melendez selected five hundred men and made every preparation for the march and battle. A small party was sent to reconnoiter and secure a native guide. They returned next day with an Indian who promised to lead them safely to the French.

"If you betray us, I will slay you," said Melendez through his interpreter.

"I will conduct you in safety," the Indian answered.

It was still raining hard, and some of the officers tried to prevail on Melendez to wait until the weather cleared a little,

"No; God commands that we act at once," he said. "We cannot slight the opportunity offered us. Besides, the storm will cover our approach; for what Frenchman would think of an attack in such weather?"

After mass, Melendez put himself at the head of the five hundred men armed with matchlocks, lances, battle-axes, swords and crossbows, and, leaving the fort in charge of his brother and the ships in charge of the vice-admiral, he set forth through the rain, guided by the Indian. The road was a path through the everglades and swamps. They could only travel in single file, and in places were compelled to build rafts or cross streams on logs. At the close of the first day they met the two Spaniards who had been rescued from slavery by Laudonnière, and who were now about to reward his kindness by betraying the fort. They might have remained neutral in the conflict, had not John Gyrot, on his return to the fort, urged them to go to the aid of their countrymen.

At first they were supposed to be Frenchmen, and Melendez was about to order their execution, when he was convinced by one that they were Spaniards.

"If Spaniards, why are you here?" he asked.

"We were many years slaves among the Indians," explained one.

"And but just escaped?"

"Our freedom was purchased by Laudonnière, the French commandant at Fort Carolinia."

"And you come from there?"

"Yes, señor."

"What is the condition of the fort?"

"Poor; you will have but little resistance. Only the sick, the women and the children were left there."

"Have none of the ships returned?"

"Three small ones managed to escape the hurricane and are now anchored at the mouth of May River."

A consultation was held in the pouring rain, and, despite the report of the Spaniards, some of the officers were opposed to advancing further.

"It is madness to proceed," said one of the captains. "The rain increases, the streams grow wider, and travel is more difficult as we advance."

"You lack courage and the zeal of a true Christian to advise a retreat at this hour," said Melendez, in a tone of rebuke.

"Admiral, the men are exhausted and hungry."

"A few hours' rest will refresh them."

"They must have food."

"There is abundance at Fort Carolinia."

Again they took up the line of march and tramped on through mud and rain until night.

Some of the bayous were so swollen that they were compelled to go long distances around them, making many miles of extra travel. When a halt was called, the men sank down on the earth exhausted, supperless, with no bed but the wet ground, no roof save the dripping branches, soothed only by the damp wind soughing among the palms. During the night, it rained in fitful showers which drenched the suffering soldiers to the skin. Melendez fared no better than his men, and all the sleep he got was while leaning against a tree.

When morning dawned, the soldiers refused to go further. Melendez was first made aware of the mutiny by the captain who led the van, reporting that his men refused to advance. The admiral hurried forward to the sullen group of soldiers, and, fixing his powerful eyes on them, demanded:

"What means this?"

"We will go no further," said one of the soldiers, who, by general consent, acted as spokesman. "We are starving and fatigued, and our only food is the wild fruit, our bed the wet ground, and every hour we are drenched with pouring rain. We are too sick and faint to fight, our powder is damp and spoiled, and we are being marched against a fort with cannon and guns to be sacrificed like sheep."

For a moment the face of Melendez was dark with

fury. He laid his hand on his sword and was almost on the point of drawing his blade and running the mutineer through the body; but Melendez was an excellent judge of human nature, and he perceived that such a course would be dangerous to his plans. The mutineers were determined, and the death of one would not overcome them. Many of the officers were in sympathy with them, and the threatened mutiny might become an open revolt. Controlling his anger, he began in a mild tone:

"Your hardships have been great; you have marched in mud and rain through an unknown wilderness, sustained by very little food; but your hardships are no greater and your sufferings no more than were endured by your countrymen under Cortez of Mexico and Pizarro in Peru. They marched into an unknown country, through cold, heat and rain; they conquered and became rich. You have no food; there is abundance at Fort Carolinia. You want shelter from the rain; there is shelter within the fort. The two Spaniards who escaped and came to us, as well as the Catholic Frenchman, assure us that there is much gold at Fort Carolinia, gathered from the Indians. There are heaps of gold in bars and ingots for every brave and faithful man who has the courage to go forward and take it. Cortez and Pizarro, with but a hand-

ful of men, marched against the serried ranks of
countless thousands, and conquered, because God
commanded them to go.   We are marching against
a handful of sick men, poorly garrisoned, and
wholly unaware of our presence.   Shame on those
who hesitate from cowardice; more shame on those
who refuse God's command.   Come!   All who
are true Spaniards, follow me, and God will protect you!"

Gradually Melendez had warmed up in his
speech, his enthusiasm swaying every heart, until,
at the close of his harangue, every soldier in the
ranks was shouting:

"On to Carolinia!   Death to the heretics!"

The army was soon again on the march, and
pressed on for four or five hours, when they were
met by Gyrot, who had come with some final
instructions and information as to the attack.

"The fort is near," he said.   "Make your attack
to-night, while all sleep, and the victory will be
easy."

"Has any rumor of our approach reached the
fort?" asked Melendez.

"No; the disappearance of the Spaniards caused
some comment; but they do not dream of an attack
by land."

"Have they ships in the harbor?"

"Three; but they are small craft, and will do you no harm."

"Have they news of Ribault?"

"No, monsieur; and they fear that he and his ships are lost at sea. Is Francisco Estevan with you?"

"No; who is he?"

"He is a Spaniard, proselyted to the Huguenot faith, and a warm friend of Laudonnière. He is no doubt a spy watching to betray you."

"In that case I would rather hang him than any other heretic."

John Gyrot then gave the Spaniards the plans of the fort, and left them to return and report that there was no enemy in the wood. Night set in, dark and rainy, and the Spaniards carefully advanced to within a few hundred paces of the fort and halted to await John Gyrot's signal. The historian hesitates to record the awful event at Fort Carolinia on that fatal September 21st, 1565.

CHAPTER XI.

A REIGN OF TERROR.

A FEELING of uneasiness pervaded the garrison at Fort Carolinia. Laudonnièrc, who had not recovered from his illness, rosc from bed and wcnt about the fort, notwithstanding his friends Challus and Le Moyne tried to keep him in out of the pelting rain.

"I cannot," hc said, "I feel an impression that all is not right. Something terriblc is going to happen. Has no news come from Ribault?"

"None."

"God pity us if wc should be attacked in our wretched condition."

"You are weak and ill, monsieur," said Le Moyne.

"It is my great responsibility—the helpless women and children I have in my keeping that makes me wrctched and anxious."

"Thero is no need to fear, monsieur. Three of the vessels have rcturned and are in the harbor.

172

These will keep the enemy from attacking by sea, and we need expect them from no other quarter."

"They may attack by land."

"Impossible, monsieur. They would never find their way across the country."

"They may have a guide."

"Who?"

"We may have a traitor among us."

"A traitor! impossible!" They all three went under a long shed on which the rain continued its unceasing patter, running off by small gutter-spouts which carried it to the ditch that drained the fort. Laudonnière, after a long silence said, "I may do wrong to call him a traitor; yet after all I have been to him it would seem ill return to betray me in my weakness."

"Of whom do you speak, monsieur?"

"A young Spaniard who was captured by the pirates and brought to the fort. I immediately gave him his liberty, and, there being no way to send him to Cuba, he made his home with me. Though a Catholic, I believed him the ideal of a true, noble man. It seems very probable that, when his countrymen came to annihilate us, he went over to them, and is now plotting against our lives."

"Whom do you mean, monsieur?"

"Francisco Estevan."

"Where is he?"

"Yes, where? He disappeared the day the Spanish fleet appeared off our coast, and only yesterday the two Spaniards, whose liberty I bought, also disappeared. I might have expected it of them; but that Francisco should be a traitor seems hardly possible."

Laudonnière could say no more. Challus and Le Moyne persuaded him to return to the house as the dampness might bring on a relapse.

At one end of the shed, crouching behind some boxes, was a slight, girlish form, her bright blue eyes dimmed with tears, and her pale face strangely agitated—Hortense De Barre had heard the unjust suspicions against Estevan. She had full faith in all the promises the young Spaniard had made, and it grieved her heart to hear him maligned while away laying and executing plans for her safety.

Laudonnière had been but a few moments in his room, when Hortense, wrapped in a cloak to protect her from the falling rain, darted across the court to his apartment. The commandant was alone, and, going to him, she said:

"Monsieur, I heard your remarks while under the shed but a few moments ago."

"What design had you, mademoiselle?"

"It was quite unintentional on my part, monsieur; but what I heard was so unjust that I must beg you to correct it."

"To what are you referring, mademoiselle?"

"You called Francisco Estevan a traitor," she said, her eyes filling with tears and her breast heaving with sobs. "He is not a spy against us."

"Whither is he gone?"

"I know not."

"Then how can you say he is not a spy?"

"He is too good, too noble to harm those he loves."

"I once thought so; but his strange absence may cause me to change my opinion."

She pleaded with Laudonnière for Francisco, telling him her assurance of his fidelity to the French people and that he would surely return soon, and explain his absence; but the grim commandant only shook his head doubtfully and told her the proofs were against him.

It was already grown dark. A servant entered the room and lighted the tapers which gave out a dim, ghastly light, showing the bare walls of logs on which hung the sword, buckler, and matchlock of Laudonnière, while in a corner stood his formidable crossbow. She realized that it was no use to plead longer with him, and left to return to the wretched hut set apart for her, when she was suddenly met at the door by Gyrot.

"Ah! mademoiselle, I have good news."

There was a fiendish light in his eyes and a demoniacal smile on his face, which she at once interpreted as meaning some disaster to Francisco.

"What do you mean?" she asked.

"I have such excellent news."

Laudonnière, who had heard the short dialogue, came to the door and asked:

"What have you to report?"

"We have seized the spy!"

"Whom?" asked both Hortense and Laudonnière.

"Francisco Estevan."

Hortense tried to speak, but her voice failed her, and she stood mute with horror, her eyes fixed on the villain.

Gyrot then told them how his suspicions had been aroused at the mysterious conduct of Estevan, and how, by watching him, he saw him in the wood negotiating with some men from the ships to betray the fort; that he was to lead them to Carolinia in three days; adding that he followed the Spaniard to the fort he intended to betray and had him arrested. The truth of the matter was, that, as Gyrot was returning from his last interview with Melendez, he reached the fort about the time Estevan arrived from a secret conference with Saturiova. His wicked mind conceived a cunning plan for the

Spaniard's destruction, and he ordered two soldiers to arrest him.

"It is false, it is all false," cried Hortense, wringing her hands.

"Bring the prisoner to me," said Laudonnière, "and I will make him confess everything."

Hortense lingered at the door, pale and trembling, as Estevan was brought a prisoner into the presence of the commandant. Estevan was in great peril; for, in those times, suspicion of treason was usually enough to secure punishment by death.

"Let me come in! Let me speak with him!" pleaded Hortense as he was taken to Laudonnière's consultation chamber; but she was excluded and Laudonnière and the prisoner were locked in the room. Thus two terrible hours passed, and Hortense, who remained in the hall, imagined that they were torturing him to death in that awful room.

The rain poured down in torrents and it was a wild, dark night. Nearly all the garrison had gone to bed; the guard stood under the shed to be out of the rain, and no one saw John Gyrot as he stole away from the commandant's house with a lighted torch in his hand. He mounted the wall of the fort and waved the torch three times in the air. At this moment there came from the intense darkness the blast of a bugle. It was followed by the report of a gun, and the guard cried:

12

"We are attacked! God defend us!"

Laudonnière, hearing the cry, locked his prisoner in his room and rushed to the defense. He buckled on his sword and seized his gun. Le Moyne and Challus joined him in the hall, and all three with drawn swords rushed out into the rain and darkness calling the garrison to arms.

The garrison was in confusion. Few could discover from whence the foe was coming. Some ran to the river-side, others to the east or north, and a few were at the point where the attack was made. Another bugle blast and a volley of bullets and bolts rained into the fort. One gallant guardsman fell, pierced by three arrows. With a deafening shout, the Spaniards came pouring over the works like devils. Never did Satan inspire fiends to more brutal butchery. Another guard, who sprang with halberd to drive them back, was knocked down and run through with lances.

Laudonniere sounded his battle-cry, and, summoning all the men he could about him, rushed against the avalanche and strove to drive them back; but might as well a house of straw be set to resist the fury of a cyclone. His men were knocked down and butchered before him, while he, Le Moyne, and Challus fought like madmen; but the avalanche still poured on. No sooner was one beaten down and wounded than a second took his place. Over the works, front and right, the horde of steel-clad demons poured. They were already in possession of the fort, though Laudonnière and a few faithful followers made a feeble resistance at the north end. Through all the dire conflict, John Gyrot stood on the rampart holding aloft the blazing torch, while the smile of a devil played on his face as he watched the butchery of his countrymen.

Having gained the south part of the fort, the Spaniards fell upon the women and children, killing them indiscriminately. The young, the old, the sick and infirm were killed in their houses, in their beds and on their knees. No prayer for mercy could avail. One child but five or six years of age fled in its night-clothes, and tried to crawl under the house, but was pulled out and slain.

The mêlée was at its height when the door of the room in which Francisco Estevan was confined was suddenly burst from its hinges, and the young Spaniard leaped into the hall where Hortense stood, pale and speechless, gazing through the open portals on the terrible scene; she seemed powerless to move. He seized her in his arms, and in a voice hoarse with emotion, gasped:

" Hortense, we must fly for our lives! "

She pointed at those bloody men; they cut down a child, they pierced a woman through the body; blood was flowing like a crimson river, and the

hellish scene was lighted by the torch of John Gyrot, who looked like a fiend from darkness.

"My God!" she groaned and sank insensible in
the young Spaniard's arms.

Estevan was strong as a giant, and, seizing the insensible maiden with his left arm, he laid hold of the
sword which had fallen from the hand of a dead
Frenchman and started toward the western gate,
from which escape seemed most probable.   He
saw John Gyrot on the rampart holding the blazing
torch aloft, and his quick perception said he was to
be avoided.   He was hurrying westward, when he
came upon a sight which he never forgot to his
dying day.   A large Frenchman was struggling
with three Spaniards who had seized him as he
rushed half dressed from his house.   In spite of
the Frenchman's struggles, his bites and his cries,
he was forced to his knees.   Then one of the
Spaniards who had a mace in his hand raised it,
and signed to his companions to. get out of the
way; they did so, and the Frenchman strove to
rise; but the mace fell with dreadful force on his
left temple.   A dull, heavy sound was heard and the
man dropped on his face.   One of the soldiers rolled
him over on his back, and, with a single stroke
of his knife, opened his throat; then, mounting
on his stomach, he stamped violently on it with his
feet, bringing forth a jet of blood from the wound.

JOHN GAROT HELD ALOFT THE BLAZING TORCH, THE SMILE OF A DEVIL
ON HIS FACE.

"God! can such men be human?" cried Estevan, hurrying with his insensible burden toward the gate.

"Here is one escaping!" cried a soldier, hurrying after him. Two more sprang forward to intercept the fugitive; but he shouted in Spanish:

"Hinder me not. I am a Spaniard and a good Catholic."

"How know we that?"

"My language would tell you that!"

"Whom have you there?"

"A Catholic who has swooned, and I am carrying her outside the fort that she may not be slain for a Huguenot."

Estevan's conscience never troubled him for the falsehood. He gained the forest with his charge in some way, he never knew exactly how. All was a wild whirlpool of excitement and confusion.

It seemed a frightful dream from which he could not awake. Into the forest, through the cold rain he plunged, staggering forward. It was so dark that eyes were of no avail. He stumbled over stones, he ran against bushes and scratched himself, tearing his flesh as well as his clothing; yet through it all he clung to the insensible Hortense for whose sake he was flying he knew not whither.

CHAPTER XII.

"NOT AS FRENCHMEN, BUT AS LUTHERANS."

ACCORDING to the Spanish chronicles, one hundred and forty-two Huguenots, mostly women and children, or sick and infirm men, were put to death that night; while the Spaniards did not lose a single man.

Many of the French who escaped into the forest perished for lack of food and clothing, or were pursued and shot by the Spaniards; while a few were captured by the Indians and made slaves.

Among those to escape the massacre in the fort and finally return to Europe were Laudonnière, Challus, and Le Moyne. A few others escaped, some of whom joined this party, and among them young Peter De Bray. The darkness of the night and their knowledge of the country, no doubt, greatly aided them. They paused on a bit of rising ground above the fort and looked down upon the place of the fearful massacre. All was dark and silent now. The dead lay stark and stiff on the ground, their pale faces and sightless eyes upturned to the beating rain.

"Whither shall we go, monsieur?" asked Le Moyne.

"If we can reach the river, we will go aboard the ships," Laudonnière answered.

"But the fort is between us and the ships."

"We must go around it."

"The night is so dark, I doubt if we can."

"Our knowledge of the country will help us; for, dark as the night is, we must make the détour of the fort and reach the ships by dawn of day."

"Our people are widely scattered."

"True; yet we must get as many together as we can. The blood-hounds will be in the forest by dawn of day."

Throughout the night the little squad of Frenchmen, whom Laudonnière collected about him, wandered through the forest, guided only by instinct, for there was not a ray of light to reveal a path to them. When day dawned, they found themselves on the banks of the river below the fort.

.、 As soon as he was master of the fort, Melendez published an order that all the women, and all the male children under fifteen years of age, should be spared, but that all others must perish. This order was not issued until the conflict had raged a long time, and many children, some of a very tender

age, had been put to death. When his proclamation was made known, many who had been hiding
came forth to give themselves up. Among those
to appeal for mercy were some men who had mis-
understood his proclamation:

"Save these Lutherans," said Melendez, when
the men came to implore his mercy. "We shall
hang them as an example to the world."

Before the conflict ended John Gyrot began to
search for Hortense. Fortunately, he had not witnessed the escape of Francisco Estevan with the
insensible Huguenot. He went to Melendez, and,
telling him of the girl's disappearance, said:

"Let your men help me to find her as soon as it
shall be light, monsieur; and I claim her when
found."

"She shall be given you for your faithful service in our cause."

"I have not been able to find the proselyte Francisco since the attack."

"Where was he before you gave the signal?"

"In consultation with the commandant, Laudonnière. He had but just returned from spying on
your army."

"He shall hang with the others!" cried Melendez.

Morning dawned on the terrible scene. Mass
was performed, prayers offered, and psalms, of
thanksgiving sung over the victory, and the

foundation of a church laid on the soil still red with the blood of the innocent.

Melendez, with a strong party, went down to the river and hailed the vessels under command of young Ribault. On being answered, the *Adelantado* summoned the crews to surrender.

"I already have your fort in my possession, and if you will peacefully surrender I will allow you to transport yourselves in any one of your ships you may choose to France; but if you do not surrender, I will put every one of you to the sword."

Young Ribault was frightened; but his officers advised him that to surrender was certain death, and he answered:

"I shall put to sea and return to France with all my vessels."

Melendez returned to the fort in a rage and commanded his men:

"Train the cannon on them, and sink the ships before they leave the river."

The artillery in the fort began to bombard the ships, and they retired beyond range of the guns.

When the ships were out of reach, Melendez said:

"We will now dispose of such of these devils as we have; bring them forth."

A large tree with great spreading branches stood

without the fort, and the male prisoners were all
hanged upon this tree, to which was affixed the
following inscription:

"These persons are not treated in this manner
because they are Frenchmen, but because they are
heretics and enemies of
God."

This was the fate of all
the Frenchmen taken at
the fort, those who sur-
rendered voluntarily, and
those who were given up
by the Indians to whom
they fled for s h e l t e r .
About twenty more who still remained in the woods were pursued and shot like so many beasts.
Fort Carolinia now lost its name,
"NOT AS FRENCH- as the Spaniards changed it to
MEN, BUT AS LU- St. Mattheo, on whose day it was
THERANS."
reduced.

At daylight Laudonnière found himself at the
head of a dozen followers. Some who had been
with him in the early part of the evening had
become separated and wandered into other parts of
the wood, among them young Peter De Bray.
They were below the fort as we have stated,
and even below the vessels before the cannon drove

them further down the stream. The ships sailed
past them; but they followed after them until they
cast anchor, when Laudonnière ventured out upon
the beach, and shouted and waved his hat to attract
the attention of his countrymen on deck.

Young Ribault saw him, and a boat was lowered,
manned, and pulled toward them. When within
fifty yards of the shore, the boat came to a halt,
and the officer in it hailed them and demanded to
know who they were.

"Laudonnière, and a dozen of his people escaped
from the massacre at the fort," the French commandant answered.

"Bring all your men on the beach that we may
see them and know that this is not a ruse of the
Spaniards," said the officer.

The men were paraded on the beach, and the
boat came quickly to the shore and conveyed the
wretched survivors to the ship of young Ribault,
who listened to the story of the massacre with
many a shudder.

"And now," said the commandant at the conclusion, "let us go in search of your father."

With a shake of his head, Ribault answered:

"No; I am going to France."

"What! return to France and desert your
father?"

"I will save my life."

"But your father's fleet may be safe, and with it we could drive them out of the country."

"If alive, my father will return to France."

"He may be wrecked on some island or on the coast, and in need of aid."

But no argument or appeal to his filial duty could alter the decision of young Ribault; he was determined to return to France at once. Laudonnière was so provoked at his cowardly decision that he would not return to Europe in the same ship with him. They sank one of their vessels because they had not men enough to sail her. Laudonnière, Challus, and Le Moyne sailed in the same ship to Europe. To the two latter, the world is indebted for an account of the horrible scenes we have related. By stress of weather they were driven to England, where Laudonnière was detained a long time by sickness. When at last he went to his own country, notwithstanding all his services, he met with a cold reception from the French king, who was then more than ever embroiled with Coligni and the Huguenots.

Melendez appointed Gonzalo de Villareal to be governor of St. Mattheo with a garrison of three hundred men, and with the remainder he returned to St. Augustine; for, having as yet no knowledge of Ribault's fate, he believed him still at sea and thought there was danger of his falling upon St.

Augustine during his absence. He was received with great pomp by his garrison, and, notwith-standing his barbarities, was extolled by his countrymen as a perfect hero, statesman and Christian gentleman. Upon his first arrival in Florida, he had taken some French prisoners whom he sent on board the *Pelagius* to be carried to Hispaniola. On the voyage the prisoners rose one night, killed the officers, mastered the crew, and sailed away to Denmark, where they disposed of the vessel.

. . . . . .

At this part of our melancholy narrative, it is necessary to return to Ribault and his miserable followers whom we left wrecked on the Florida coast. All his fleet save the three mentioned in May River were wrecked on the coast near Cape Canaveral. Their condition was wretched; they were without provisions or weapons; their scanty clothing was torn and soaked with ocean brine, and they were in a wild, inhospitable country. .

A council was held to determine what should be done.

"We must return to Fort Carolinia," Ribault declared.

"It is a long distance," said Cossel.

"Great as is the distance, we must return or perish."

Little did they dream of the calamity that had

befallen Fort Carolinia. With only the sun to guide them by day and the stars by night, their food wild fruit, berries, and turtles' eggs, they set out up the coast, picking up other shipwrecked and wretched comrades as they advanced.

One day they discovered an empty sloop on the coast. It had belonged to the Spaniards, and was blown away in the hurricane and beached. Save that some of the yards were sprung a little, it was in good condition. They set to work to repair it, and soon had it ready for sea. At high tide the sloop was launched, manned, and given in charge of Vasseur with orders to go and search for the river May.

Vasseur sailed on his voyage, and the Frenchmen left behind, although weary with travel and half famished for food, continued their journey up the coast. Vasseur returned in four or five days, and, putting into the little bay where Ribault had halted his despondent men, went ashore. As Ribault went to meet him he saw nothing reassuring in his features.

"Have you found the fort, Vasseur?" asked Ribault.

"Yes, monsieur."

"What did you see?"

"The Spanish flag flies over it."

"Then it has fallen!"

"It certainly has."

Ribault felt his heart sink within him.

"Better had we all perished in the hurricane. Did you see any of our vessels?"

"No, monsieur."

His men were starving and clamored to be taken to Fort Carolinia.

"We know not what treatment we will receive if we fall into the hands of the Spaniards," pleaded Ribault.

"Would it not be well to send two officers to Melendez and ascertain what treatment we will receive if we surrender?" suggested Trenchant.

Ribault adopted the plan, and sent Cossel and Trenchant to Fort Carolinia; but they halted at St. Augustine and were agreeably surprised to meet John Gyrot there.

"What has become of the people at Fort Carolinia?" Trenchant asked.

"They were all put on board vessels and sent to France under the order of Melendez," Gyrot answered.

"Why did you not go with them?"

"The Spanish commandant was very kind to me, and out of compassion for my countrymen who were wandering about in the forests I resolved to remain, search for them, and send them home," the hypocrite answered.

Gyrot learned from his countrymen that Ribault
had been wrecked on the coast and assured them
they would receive good treatment at the hands of
Melendez.   He went to the Spanish commandant
and told him what he had learned, and those two
then and there hatched up a plan which would
have made the devil himself blush.   Melendez
came to see Trenchant and Cossel and told them
how he had sent Laudonnière and his garrison to
France in a goodly ship, and said that if Ribault
could surrender, he would give him and his followers the same terms.

As they were about to depart, John Gyrot took
Trenchant aside, and, with a smile on his sharp,
pale features, said:

"Assure our people they need not fear Melendez;
he is very kind and his only wish is to remove
them from the country."   The two embassadors
returned and reported; but the Frenchmen were
still divided in their opinion.   No one had much
faith in John Gyrot, and all knew how meritorious
the Spaniards held it to not keep faith with heretics.
Trenchant was sent back and procured a written
promise, almost as sacred as an oath, that if the
French would come in and surrender they should
not be harmed, but would be furnished with a
vessel and all needful supplies to carry them to
France.   They had the wilderness and starvation

on one side, and the solemn obligation of Melendez on the other; there could be no doubt which they would choose. Some of the starving men declared they preferred assassination to starvation in the forest.

Chaloupes were sent to convey them across the river. Ribault and Ottigny with one hundred and fifty men went first, and, as soon as they landed, were seized and bound with cords.

"Is this keeping faith?" the indignant Ribault cried. "Where is Melendez?"

"He is not here, señor," answered his guard.

The French were made prisoners as fast as they landed. Ribault was in despair until he saw Gyrot among the Spaniards, and, calling to him, he asked:

"What is the meaning of this? I am promised, on the oath of Melendez, protection and safe transportation to France, and as soon as I reach shore I am seized and bound."

"It will all be right, monsieur," assured Gyrot.

"Where is Melendez?"

"He will be here soon."

"Will you go and bring him?"

"I will."

Gyrot hurried away and took care not to return again to his wretched countrymen. A Spanish soldier, approaching Ribault, gravely asked:

13

"Do you expect French soldiers under you to obey orders, señor?"

"Without a doubt," Ribault answered.

"Then," said the soldier, "you are not to be surprised if I obey my general's orders, likewise."

So saying, he plunged his long, keen dagger into Ribault's heart. The Frenchman fell without a groan, and as Ottigny turned his eyes on his dead commander, he, too, was stabbed and fell dead across Ribault's body.

The Spanish soldiers now fell upon the French everywhere. Some were gathered together, blindfolded and shot. None were spared, save a few workmen who were kept to work on the fortifications at St. Augustine. About two hundred French, who had escaped and fled up the river May, began the construction of a fort. Most of these were Catholics, and, learning of that fact, Melendez promised them good treatment if they would return and surrender. They did so a few weeks later, and Melendez kept his word with them.

The number of Huguenots slain in this massacre has been variously estimated. It was sufficient to put a blight on Melendez throughout all time. John Gyrot, whose diabolical conduct had endeared him to Melendez, asked permission to go to the

"DO YOU EXPECT FRENCH SOLDIERS UNDER YOU TO OBEY ORDERS, SEÑOR?"

woods with a party of soldiers to search for Hortense De Barre, whom he determined should not escape him. His request was granted; but his search was futile, as we shall see.

CHAPTER XIII.

FRANCISCO ESTEVAN shuddered as he pressed the senseless, dripping girl to his breast. Their flight had been through a field of death, and perhaps some flying missile had pierced her body.

"O God! is she dead? is she dead?" groaned Francisco. It was too dark for him to see, and he thought the water dripping from her wet garments might be red with blood.

"Hortense! Hortense!" he groaned, "speak just one word to tell me you forgive me for being a Spaniard!"

The inanimate mass in his arms seemed to move. He uttered a low cry of joy, and again breathed her name in accents of love. Once more she evinced unmistakable signs of life. He sat down under a great oak, whose wide-spreading branches partially protected them from the dripping rain, and, holding her close to his heart to instil warmth in her cold form, he whispered:

"Hortense, speak!"

A slight shudder, and then a faint whisper from those lips which he could not see.

"Hortense! Hortense!"

"It is dark—so dark," she gasped. "I am cold and damp."

"Have no fear, Hortense, I will take care of you. Do you know where we are?"

"Monsieur Estevan," she murmured.

"Don't you remember?"

"Yes, yes—the fort—the wild night—the massacre. How did I escape?"

"I brought you away."

"And where are we now?"

"In the forest; I am taking you to a place of safety."

"Was it Melendez?"

"Yes."

"How many escaped?"

"I know of none save yourself. Can you forgive such devil's work?"

"As I hope to be forgiven, I forgive."

"Your religion is better than mine."

After a feeble effort, she rose to her feet.

"Are you strong enough to stand?" he asked.

"I believe so, though I am still weak. Tell me, monsieur, where are we going?"

"To a place I have provided for you in the home of an Indian chief."

"Is it far?"

"We may reach his village to-morrow. If you are not strong enough to walk, I will carry you."

"My strength is returning and in a moment I will be able to walk."

The wind sighed through the wet branches and swept the rainy sky. All the terrible sounds of a stormy night in a tropical forest fell on the ear of the startled girl, and she instinctively clung to her protector. Travel through the swamps and forests of Florida was at that day attended with no little danger, even in daylight; but on such a night as this, when every bayou and swamp contained a thousand lurking foes, where the wild beast, driven from his lair by the rising water, sought a victim on which to vent his rage, when the earth beneath, the heavens above, and the forest about them seemed charged with deadly fury, it was enough to intimidate the stoutest heart.

"You must be as brave as you were on the night you rescued me from the wreck," whispered Estevan.

"I will depend on you," she answered.

"God give me strength to protect you. Are you strong enough to go on?"

"I am. How far are we from the fort?"

"Not far. I have no idea of the distance I

struggled with you, but it could not have been more than three-fourths of a mile."

"Is it over there?"

"It is," he answered sadly. "All is still there now."

She shuddered and said she would try to walk. Supporting her with his arm, they went slowly through the dripping wood, Estevan feeling his way with the naked sword he had brought from the fort. They had not gone more than a mile, when he suddenly came to a halt and whispered:

"I hear voices."

She asked in what direction.

"On our left, between us and the fort."

"Perhaps friends are coming."

"No, señorita, it cannot be," he answered. "They were all slain; but have no fear; I will protect you as long as I live."

"Could they find us in the darkness?" she asked.

"The Spaniards sometimes hunt fugitives with blood-hounds; but, even if Melendez has brought dogs with him, the rain, which is so discomforting to us, will prove a blessing in obliterating the trail by which the ferocious beasts would have followed us."

They stood very still behind some trees, while the voices drew nearer. It was too dark to see;

but the tramp of feet and low voices warned them
that a considerable party was coming toward them.
Francisco's only hope was that the party would
turn aside before they were discovered. The
fugitives dared not speak a word even in a whisper, but crouched against the tree scarcely breathing. A single flash of lightning would reveal
their hiding-place; but Heaven seemed kind, and
held the sable cloak of night unriven about them.

The party, evidently a dozen in number, passed
so near to the fugitives, that they could almost
touch them. Singularly enough, not a word was
spoken by the wanderers. That band of stragglers
was Laudonnière and his followers on their way to
the ships, and a single word would have told the
hiding, breathless fugitives that they were friends.
Their discovery would have resulted in an entire
change in the life of Hortense, and saved her long
years of hopeless misery; but fate plays strange
pranks sometimes, and this party of friends, whom
they supposed to be enemies, passed on. Estevan
waited until they were out of hearing, and, assuring himself that no others were near, asked:

"Can you walk now? The way is once more
clear."

"I can walk, monsieur."

They resumed their journey, carefully picking
their way over the muddy ground, through swamps

and over fallen trees. Travel was necessarily slow
and painful, as they were compelled to grope their
way. Estevan used his sword as a blind man
does his cane. Despite his caution, he once missed
his footing and both plunged down an embankment
into a deep lake. Never losing his wonderful presence of mind, he rescued Hortense and himself
from drowning, but lost his sword in the effort,
and, wholly unarmed, they wandered on. He
broke a stick with which he felt his way. Though
the rain still fell, the fury of the tempest was
past, and the showers were only the spasmodic
throes of a dying storm. A still greater blessing
was promised in the birth of a new day. Already
the eastern horizon was growing lighter, and before
long the wretched fugitives could see to travel
through the wood without the aid of a cane.
Brighter and brighter grew the wood, until it was
once more light. The rain ceased, the soft gray
rolled away from the sky, and the sun rose in its
golden splendor; but its light revealed a shadow
of woe. Two homeless fugitives were wandering
helplessly through the labyrinthian mazes of a
tropical forest, without a ray of joy or hope on
their faces. The rain-drops glistened like pearls
from the fragrant orange-blossoms, the flowers
lifted their heads brightly along the way, the
sweet songs of the oriole and mocking-bird made

the air musical; but all these awakened no feeling of happiness in the fair Huguenot. She saw only the wild struggle and heard only the groans of her dying people. Hortense

"SHE WENT WHITHERSOEVER FRANCISCO LED."

was benumbed with horror. She could not weep, for tears were denied her, and with her head meekly bowed, looking like some nymph or dryad of the forest lost to life, she went whithersoever Francisco led.

"Are you tired?" he asked.

"I don't know."

"Are you hungry?"

"I have no thought for food."

"I can pluck some wild fruit."

"No; go on," she answered. "I have no desire for fruit." Then she asked, "How far are we now from Fort Carolinia?"

"It must be several miles."

"Do you see any of the Spaniards?"

"No; we are free from pursuit for the present, and before nightfall we will be in the village of Saturiova."

She seldom spoke after this, save when addressed.

She was patient and uncomplaining, enduring the fatigue with scarce a murmur. They frequently paused to rest, and once he proposed to make her a bed of leaves that she might sleep and recuperate her strength. She fixed her sad blue eyes on him and said she could not sleep.

The sun was low when the village of Saturiova was reached. The chief was sitting in front of his lodge, as if expecting them. Their wretched condition roused no visible sympathy in the breast of the stern old warrior, nor did he express any emotion at their terrible story.

Hortense, who knew nothing of the aborigines, felt her heart sink in despair. This indifferent savage seemed as unconcerned as a stone and would undoubtedly refuse them protection. Francisco kept on, despite the apparent unconcern of the chief, concluding with:

"Saturiova, I have brought the pale lily whom the Spaniards would slay to make her home with you for a while, until the storm has blown away. Will you take her and treat her as your own daughter? She is young, unaccustomed to rude scenes such as she has witnessed, and to you she appeals for shelter and sympathy."

This speech being in the Indian tongue, Hortense of course did not comprehend a word of it. The chief was moved as only a chief can be, and, rising, he approached the trembling girl, and, taking both her hands in his own, answered:

"I will take the white lily from across the great water to my lodge, and she shall be my daughter. She shall share the wigwam with my other daughter, she shall have the best of care and Saturiova will defend her with his life."

When Francisco had translated his words, Hortense gazed up into the face so fixed and apparently immovable a few moments before, but now all beaming with kindness, and tears started to her eyes.

"Oh, thank you! thank you! and God will surely bless you," she cried.

The chief then called his daughter, a beautiful forest maiden, whose costume of gay feathers and fine fabrics denoted the rank of a princess, and gave Hortense into her keeping. The Indian maiden placed her arms affectionately about the poor fugitive and, with a smile which semed born in Heaven, murmured in her own rich tongue:

"Sister."

With a cry of joy Hortense De Barre fell on the neck of her olive-cheeked sister and wept. The Indian princess conducted her to her own lodge and left her there, while she brought the best food in the village and fed her with her own hands.

When Estevan had told Saturiova all the details of the massacre, the chief asked:

"Why do white people kill each other?"

"It is on account of religion."

"Does your God command you to do this?"

Estevan was silent. He knew that God had said, "Thou shalt not kill."

After a moment's hesitation, he answered:

"The people from France are heretics."

"Do you worship the same God?"

"Yes."

"Then why do you kill each other? We who worship different Gods never fight over religion, but for slaves, land, bread, or power. Your religion is not so good as ours if it makes people so cruel."

"While we worship the same God, the Huguenot denies the infallibility of the pope, or the power of the priest to forgive sins, or that the bread and wine of the sacrament is the true flesh and blood of Christ, and they refuse to believe in the Virgin as intercessor with Christ."

The old chief heard him to the end and asked:

"It was for that your people killed them? You won't even let them worship the God you worship, unless they worship Him your way? Is this what you boast of as civilization?"

Francisco struggled hard to maintain his position; but the chief, with his practical common sense, propounded many puzzling questions, which gave the young Romanist food for thought. It was late in the evening before the Spaniard thought of retiring, and he expressed a wish to know that Hortense was well cared for before going to the lodge set apart for him.

"Come with me," said the chief, and, taking up a lighted pine knot, he led the way to his daughter's lodge. He pulled aside the opening, and, holding the torch so as to throw the reflection within, said:

"Look."

Francisco Estevan glanced within, and on a bed

of the softest dressed skins placed on dry, clean rushes covered with European blankets, lay the white and red sister, clasped in each other's arms, sleeping the sweet sleep of innocence. Francisco's eyes grew moist at this evidence of trust and affection.

"Have you any fear for the white lily?" asked Saturiova, closing the opening of the lodge.

"No."

He then bade the old chief adieu and went to the lodge set apart for him. Francisco slept the sleep of exhaustion, and awoke late next morning. The old chief had him called to breakfast. He inquired about Hortense and learned that she had slept well and would soon be out of the lodge. It was a calm, sweet morning. It seemed as if no storm had ever swept over the sky which smiled in peace on the blooming forest, and but for the bitter recollections of two nights ago, Estevan might have been happy. The village of Saturiova was most romantically and delightfully situated on a slight elevation, surrounded by orange groves whose perfume burdened the air.

When Hortense came from the lodge she was greatly improved by her night's rest, though still pale, with the look of horror and fear not gone from her face. She met Francisco joyfully, and he led her to a rustic seat under the trees.

"Can you be happy here?" he asked.

"I will try," she answered.

"You must stay here for the present, at least, until I can go to Melendez and secure his promise to spare you."

"Do you dare go to him?" she asked.

"Why not? I am a Spaniard and a Catholic; I am consecrated to the priesthood and he dare not bring his thunderbolt of vengeance on my head."

She shuddered, but remained silent. He noticed the sad look on her face and said:

"Hortense—sister—do you hate the Spaniards?"

"No; I hope God will forgive them."

"Can you?"

"Yes."

"You are an angel, and may the blessed Virgin guard and watch over you!" cried the enraptured Estevan.

"What will you do?" she asked, after a few moments of silence.

"I am going to return at once to the fort and seek out Melendez. My father knew him, and I shall presume on their acquaintance to ask a favor at his hands."

"And leave me here alone?" she asked sadly and plaintively.

"Are you afraid to be left alone?"

"No; but you are the only one on whom I can depend for safety now."

"I will not desert you, sister. As you saved my life I will save yours; as you remained my truest friend in my hour of distress, I will remain faithful to you, and though I go away it is for your own good. Have you any fears to remain here?"

"None. My red sister's father has promised me his protection, and I have heard that an Indian chief will keep his word."

With gentle words and wholesome counsel he soothed her fears, until her mind became once more tranquil, and he left her leaning on her red sister, whom she had already learned to love. Her resignation and forgiving spirit had opened the mind and heart of the young priest to a new idea of Christianity. When he contemplated the heinous work of his own people, he was constrained to ask:

"Can love of God make devils of men? When I reflect on that scene I almost despise my monastic vows."

Going to Saturiova, he took the old chief's hand in both his own, and, in a voice which trembled with emotion, said:

"I am going away, Saturiova, to be gone, I know not how long. Guard my sister with your life; she is very precious to me."

14

CHAPTER XIV.

THE return of Estevan to Fort Carolinia was like a solemn pilgrimage. Early one morning he came in sight of the fort and saw his country's flag flying over it and observed Spanish soldiers moving about the works; but the sight inspired no feeling of joy in his breast. A long ridge of fresh earth just outside the wall showed where the dead slept, while hanging from the branches of a great tree, beneath whose friendly shade he had so often reposed, were frightful objects suspended by the necks, with faces blackened and bodies swollen, until, as they swayed in the air, one could hardly realize that those revolting things had ever been human beings. The air about them was impregnated with a foul stench, and hordes of black and green flies swarmed around them, while above soared the loathsome vulture. Unable to bear the sight, Estevan covered his face with his hands, and, uttering a prayer for strength, ran past the tree toward the fort.

When within a few yards of the gate, he was challenged by the sentry, who demanded to know who he was and whence he came. He answered: "I am a Spaniard. I came from the forest, and I want to see Melendez."

"I believe you to be a heretic," answered the guard, "and if you should prove to be one we will hang you to yonder tree. Behold, we daily increase their number."

"I am what I say, and can prove my assertion," he answered.

"Why are you in this country? you came not with us."

"I am Francisco Estevan, a native of Cuba, and was on my way from Spain, where I had been studying for the monastery, when my ship was seized by some French pirates who brought me to this colony."

An officer of the guard came up at this moment and consulted a short time with the sentry, and then ordered Francisco to approach.

"You say you are a Spaniard?" asked the officer.

"I am."

"Your language denotes Spanish; are you a good Catholic?"

"I am."

"Whom do you wish to see?"

"The commandant Melendez."

"Melendez is not commandant; he has appointed Gonzalo de Villarael governor of St. Mattheo, while he returned to St. Augustine."

"Is Mendoza here?"

"He departed with Melendez."

"I must see Melendez, for my business is with him."

He was sent to Gonzalo de Villarael, who regarded him with suspicion and asked him a great many questions. Francisco frankly answered all of them; but took care to say nothing of the hiding-place of Hortense.

"You say you come from the forest: have you seen any Huguenots?"

"No."

"Some are hiding in the woods."

"I have met with none."

"Are you friendly to the French Huguenots?"

"They are the enemies of the Catholic religion."

"Have you not espoused theirs?"

Francisco was thunderstruck at the question, and, bounding to his feet, asked:

"Do you mean to ask if I have become a Huguenot?"

"I do."

"No."

"It was reported that you were a proselyte to their faith before our arrival."

"Señor, you have heard falsely." ·

"At any rate I must detain you a prisoner, though we shall not hang you until we have more proof."

Francisco could hardly believe his senses. Staring at the Spanish governor, he exclaimed:

"A prisoner! I, a prisoner!"

"Yes, señor, you are a prisoner."

"I demand, then, to be taken to Melendez."

"Your request shall be granted; you shall be taken to Melendez, but not now, we have no time. For the next few days we will confine you at St. Matthco; but as soon as a guard can be spared, you will be removed to St. Augustine."

A few days! Then for days, he knew not how many, he was to be kept away from Hortense, who, in her strange home in the wilderness, surrounded by wild, savage people to whom she could not speak a word, would day by day watch and wait with heart-breaking anxiety for his return. Perhaps he would never return. Some one had maligned him to the Spanish officers, and that one, his instincts told him, was John Gyrot. The wily devil had planned well, and Francisco had fallen into the trap he had prepared. He was unable to drive from his mind the recollection of those horrible things he had seen suspended from the tree, and knew that he might soon add another to the list.

In the darkest dungeon the fort could afford Francisco Estévan was confined. He could take no heed of the flight of time, for night and day were alike to him in his dismal cell. Here he pined and waited, and hoped and dreamed of Hortense, exposed to all the nameless horrors of the wilderness. Ten days passed before he was brought forth from his dungeon to meet the governor, and then all the satisfaction he could get was that he was to be sent to St. Augustine. Pale and silent, yet with a burning fire within his breast, Estevan meekly submitted. What had he ever done to his countrymen to merit such treatment? He asked no questions, for they would not be answered. He was placed in charge of a guard of twenty soldiers and sent to St. Augustine. The rains had ceased, the earth was dry, and the forest through which they journeyed beautiful as only a Floridian forest in that land of eternal Spring can be. The prisoner was in no mood to enjoy his beautiful surroundings and the songs of tropical birds.

The march to St. Augustine was a journey in silence, and the prisoner, whose hopes grew fainter every day, was relieved when they came in sight of the fort at the close of the third day's march. A prison had been built at St. Augustine. The first thought of the Europeans in settling in the New World was the construction of prisons. Francisco was conducted at once to the dungeon, as it was too late to see the governor that day.

He consoled himself with the thought that Balboa and Cortez had both been in prison, and both had escaped to become rulers of men. Would fate grant the same fortune to him? His mind was so wholly occupied with the lonely girl in the wigwam of the savages that he gave little thought to himself.

Next morning the guard came and escorted the prisoner, heavily ironed, from his dungeon to the governor's hall. On the way he was somewhat amazed to meet John Gyrot. The malignant grin on his face denoted a fiendish triumph.

"Monsieur Estevan, I greet you. Good-morning!"

With a look of supreme contempt, Estevan answered:

"It is you I have to thank for this."

"Monsieur, don't be too hard on me."

"I plainly see your cunning hand and fertile brain in all the misfortunes which have befallen me; but a day of reckoning will come. Of that be assured."

"I would be monsieur's friend if he would let me, I would be his great friend."

"My friend? Have you influence with Me-lendez?"

"Not a great deal; just a little. Nevertheless, such as I have shall be used in your interest, if you will aid me."

"You demand a return?"

"Not much, monsieur. All I require of you is to inform me where Mademoiselle De Barre is hiding. I have no evil intentions toward the mademoiselle; but, being an old and respected friend of the family, I naturally feel a great interest in her. She may be in danger, and in need of a friend. Gyrot is her devoted friend."

Turning to the guard, Estevan asked to be taken at once to Melendez. Strangely enough, the guard did not stir, and Gyrot, who seemed to exercise authority over them, continued: "During the conflict, monsieur fled from the fort and mademoiselle was also missing. Then where were they? No doubt they went together."

He was bland, smiling, and polite, and, withal, deceitful. Estevan, disdaining to hold further conversation with one whom he had detested from the hour he had first seen his ugly face, again appealed to the guard.

"Will you take me to Melendez?"

"Don't be hasty, monsieur," continued Gyrot with his malignant grin. "Stay until I have feasted

my eyes on that dear friend whom I saved from
the pirates. Tell me, where is the mademoiselle?"

"I will not talk with you. My business is
with the admiral," Francisco answered.

"So you will not answer me. Perhaps you pre-
fer to answer the admiral," and, with a polite wave
of his hand, Gyrot signalled the guard to move on
with their prisoner.

He was conducted to Melendez, who was evidently expecting him. The wild-eyed fanatic who
had been commissioned to deeds of blood gazed on
the prisoner without the least show of sympathy.
After a moment's silence, he said in his terrible
voice:

"You have been sent to me on serious charges."

"Charges? I was not aware I was accused of
anything."

"Why did you suppose you were sent to prison?"

"I supposed it a mistake, admiral."

Melendez then read the indictment to the prisoner, charging him with sedition, heresy, treason
to the crown of Spain, apostasy, aiding and abetting
and giving comfort to the Huguenots and enemies
of the Catholic faith.

"What answer do you make?" asked Melendez
when the entire list had been read.

"I have been maligned and it is a tissue of falsehoods from beginning to end."

"Let us see if it is all false. Where were you on the night of the attack on Fort Carolinia?"

"A prisoner in the fort."

"On what charge?"

"Of being a spy and aiding and abetting my countrymen."

"That is your story. There was no record found in the fort of the charge."

"It was an informal arrest and no charge had been reduced to writing."

"What became of you during the flight?"

"I escaped."

Glancing toward the door, Francisco discovered the face of Gyrot, who had entered with his usual noiseless tread.

"You left during the battle?" continued Melendez.

"I did."

"Whither did you go?"

"To the forest."

"Alone?"

Estevan started. Melendez had, with the adroitness of an expert, led gradually up to the vital point of the case, and now his eyes were on the young Spaniard as if he would read his heart.

"Answer; did you go away alone?"

"No."

"Who accompanied you in your flight?"

"Hortense De Barre."

"A Huguenot maiden?"

"Yes."

The face of the admiral was dark and sinister, and his eyes flashed with fire, as, fixing them on the prisoner, he said:

"My orders are that all Huguenots, male and female, shall come in and surrender, and that every one knowing where a Huguenot is concealed shall reveal the hiding-place."

After waiting for several moments for the prisoner to speak, the admiral again spoke:

"I command you to tell me the whereabouts of Hortense De Barre!" He was still silent. "Will you tell, señor?"

"No, admiral, I will not."

"Then I swear by all the saints in the calendar you shall go back to that dungeon at St. Mattheo and remain there until your hair is white and your frame bent with age!" cried the enraged admiral.

"Hold, admiral! before you pass that cruel sentence let me explain."

"Speak, and I will listen."

"I want to go back to the time when I was a student in Spain, preparing for the monastery. With some monks I set out to make a pilgrimage to Rome. We went by sea and our vessel was wrecked on the coast of France, and I, of all the

crew and passengers, was rescued from death by
a French maiden. I was taken from the wreck in
an insensible condition and nursed back to life by
this good angel, but for whom I would have perished. When I recovered, I registered a vow that
should she ever be in distress I would befriend her.
Fortuitous circumstances, a little more than a
fortnight since, gave me that opportunity. I was
in Fort Carolinia as I have stated. My preserver
was there also, and the Spaniards were storming
the place; then I seized her and carried her to a
place of safety where she is to-day, admiral, hiding from John Gyrot, her persecutor from her
childhood, whose hands are red with the blood of
his countrymen, and who will not hesitate to betray
you if his interests demand it. He it is who asks
the return of Hortense De Barre. Admiral, swear
to me on the crucifix, on your honor as a Spaniard
to Spaniard, Catholic to Catholic, that Hortense De
Barre shall be free from the persecutions of John
Gyrot and accorded the same safety as other Huguenot women, and I will bring her to you!"

Melendez fixed his eyes on Gyrot as if asking
him for a reply to the charges. The wily Frenchman was already roused, for he saw danger to his
pet scheme, and, advancing nearer to the admiral,
he began:

"Monsieur has spoken with an oily tongue, and

his eloquence and falsehoods are dangerous to the
unthinking, but harmless to the man who can dis-
cern the truth. Monsieur Estevan 'was in Fort
Carolinia when news reached it of the arrival of
the Spanish fleet. If he was the good Spaniard
and Catholic which he claims to be, why did he
not go to his countrymen? He was not seized by
the Huguenots then nor imprisoned. Why? Because he was a proselyte to their faith and they had
no fear of his betraying them. Had he wished,
he could have gone to his people and told them of
the weak places in the enemy's fort and where to
strike the enemies of the holy church. Who came
to you, admiral, who gave you the plans of the
fort, and finally led you to successful victory? It
was not Francisco Estevan. Who remained with
you during the fight and held the torch to light you
on to victory? Verily, not the monsieur, but I.
The admiral will remember a sacred compact he
made with myself. I asked that he spare only
one, Hortense De Barre, a friend of my childhood.
I have kept my oath, Fort Carolinia is yours,
admiral; now will you forget your solemn obligation?"

Gyrot had Melendez in his power, for the oath
taken on the crucifix before the fall of Fort Carolinia would be kept. He assured Gyrot that he
remembered his obligation and had no disposition

to violate it; then turning to the prisoner, he added:

"You must reveal the hiding-place of Hortense De Barre."

"I cannot."

"You must."

"I will not, unless the admiral will swear on the crucifix that she shall be protected from John Gyrot."

"I can make no such oath."

"Then I will not reveal her hiding-place. I am your prisoner; do with me as you will, hang me, burn me at the stake, or put me to the rack, but, by the mother of Jesus, I swear I will not reveal her place of concealment."

Both Melendez and Gyrot were startled by the stubborn refusal of Francisco. The smile faded from the Frenchman's white face, and his eyes gleamed with an evil light.

"Monsieur is defiant, admiral; beware, or he may displace you as Vasco Nunez de Balboa did Bachelor Encisco."

For a few moments Melendez contemplated the prisoner in silence; finally he asked:

"Is this your answer?"

"It is."

"Will nothing change you?"

"Nothing."

"Guards, take him back to the dungeon and fasten him in the most secure cell."

"Hold!" cried Estevan, as the guards advanced to lead him away. "I claim the benefit of clergy; my person is sacred." .

"Have you ever been ordained?" asked Melendez.

"No."

"Clergy is denied you; you must go to St. Mattheo, where the prison is more secure."

"I demand to see Father Mendoza."   •

"He is not here."   •

"Do you deny me the right to consult a priest?"

"Mendoza is not here."

"Must I go to prison without seeing him?"

"There is no help for it. You refuse to obey the command of the king's officers, and you are charged with crimes which may cost you your life. Guards, take him back to Fort St. Mattheo and tell the governor it is my command that he be confined in the most secure cell of his prison, that he see no one and converse with no one unless by my written order. Away!"

Francisco had played his last card, and his heart sank within him. Gyrot approached the prisoner and, with a triumphant smile on his face, said:

"Give yourself no uneasiness on account of the mademoiselle. I will care for her. Sufficient soldiers will be furnished me to scour every forest glade in Florida to find her."

Francisco, without making any answer, marched away in silence to St. Mattheo, which was reached in due time. There he was confined in the most gloomy cell in the prison. Once alone, his manhood deserted him and he broke down and wept.

Day by day he hoped that Father Mendoza would call on him; but as weeks and months glided by and he came not, the prisoner reached the correct conclusion that the priest was not aware of his captivity.

Francisco exhausted all human resources, and then turned to God. All his pious ideas, which in the late tumult of events had been almost forgotten, returned. He remembered all the prayers he had been taught, and discovered a new meaning in every word. He prayed, and, no longer terrified at the sound of. his voice, prayed aloud. He laid every action of his life before the Almighty, proposed tasks to accomplish, and concluded every prayer with:

"'Forgive us our trespasses as we forgive them that trespass against us.'"

But despite all his earnest invocations, Francisco remained a prisoner. Then a gloomy feeling took possession of him. His mind was filled with his wrongs and the wrongs to that innocent girl who might be suffering more than he. His mind, constantly harassed with doubts and fears, missed the pleasure which solitude has brought to some great souls in prison. Day and night his mind was filled with Hortense in the wilderness. He was young, just in the morning of life as it were; but his mind had been well stored with useful knowledge, which, had not the wrongs of Hortense crowded out all other reflections, might have furnished him with food for pleasant thoughts. His energetic spirit was imprisoned like an eagle in a cage.

Thus the months rolled by. A year and more had passed, and he had seen no one save his jailer who brought him the miserable food that kept soul and body together.

Though scarcely able to note the flight of time, he knew that more than a year had passed since he left the little trusting girl in the forest with the assurance that he would return soon. What had been her fate? He would have given his miserable life to know that she was safe and happy.

15

CHAPTER XV.

A FAMOUS modern novelist says, "God may seem, sometimes, to forget for a while, whilst justice reposes; but there always comes a moment when He remembers." God's vengeance is as sure to fall as His mercy is to be extended. The unrepentant rebel may be spared for a while, to give him an opportunity to reform; yet he who persists in sin and folly will come to ruin in the end. What is true of individuals is also true of nations. Spain, at this period, one of the greatest, if not the greatest power on earth, was extending her dominion over the richest parts of the New World. She poured the wealth of Mexico and Peru into her coffers; but the treasure made her people rich and indolent, at the same time exciting the envy of the world, so that, in time, she paid the penalty of her cruel conquests by loss of possessions and diminution of power, until she has become one of the feeblest nations of Europe. In justice to Spain, we are compelled to say that, cruel as she was, she was little behind France in barbarity.

In the Huguenot extermination in Florida, Melendez, according to good authority, seems to have
acted in concert with the court of France, which
considered the Huguenots of Florida as the very
worst of rebels and traitors. Though they had
been settled under the charter and by the authority
of the French king CHARLES IX., he acted toward
his Protestant subjects in France much the same
as did Melendez to those in Florida. All Europe
was amazed, that, in whatever light the king might
view the Floridian Huguenots, he did not resent
the insult done to his own dignity; and all that
has been said in vindication of his tameness is that
his connections at that time did not admit of his
coming to an open rupture with Spain.

In vain patriotic Frenchmen, both Catholic and
Protestants, tried to rouse the king to action.
Coligni, the great Protestant champion, was deserted by his sovereign and the king's inhuman
mother.

Catharine de Medici, with a strange perversion
of a mother's natural instincts, after she became
regent, plunged her children, in the flower of their
youth, into a whirl of sensual pleasure, that soon
weakened their minds and bodies beyond recovery,
as she intended. When her royal son reached his
majority, he seemed incapable of resisting any
temptation which his mother placed before him, and

while he wore the crown, she ruled France. Failing in her plot to bring the Duke of Guise to the
scaffold, she, by a bit of diplomacy more cunning
than honest, changed her tactics and joined the
league against the Huguenots, of which he was
leader.   Thus we see Coligni stripped of his
power and unable to avenge the blood of his slain
colony.   We should state here that, at the massacre on the Eve of St. Bartholomew, August,
1572, when the king ordered all the Huguenots in
France to be put to death, the gallant Coligni was
the first martyr.   A band of murderers, under a
German assassin named Behme, in the employ of
the Duke of Guise, entered the admiral's room,
plunged a boar-spear to his heart, and flung his body
out of the window into the court below, where the
Duke of Guise was awaiting the consummation of
the crime.

  The slaughtered Huguenots were avenged, however, in a very extraordinary manner by a Catholic
gentleman, the Chevalier De Gourges, a soldier of
fortune and good family.   He had distinguished
himself during the wars against Spain in Italy,
where he was once captured by the enemy and
chained as a slave to a galley.   This galley was
subsequently taken by the Turks, and, shortly
after, again captured by the Maltese, who liberated
De Gourges.   He subsequently made some voyages

to Africa, Brazil, and other places, and, upon his return to France, was looked upon as the ablest navigator in Europe. A life of wild adventure and a frame seasoned to hardships made De Gourges an admirable person to carry out any desperate plan of conquest and adventure. Hearing of the massacre of his countrymen in Florida, he immediately laid a plan for avenging them and driving their murderers out of that fine country.

In order to carry out his designs, he converted all his property into ready money, and also secured long loans. With these funds he built three frigates, on board of which he put one hundred and fifty soldiers and volunteers, most of them gentlemen, besides eighty sailors. His ships drew but little water, and were so constructed that in a calm they might be worked with sweeps, by which means they could enter the mouths of rivers.

All this required time, and it was not until August, 1567, that his armament and complement of men was complete. This was nearly two years after the massacre in Florida. At last all was in readiness, and on August 22, 1567, he weighed anchor and sailed on his desperate venture. Hitherto his purpose had been kept secret from all the world, and he had obtained from M. De Moutluc, the French king's lieutenant in Gascogny, a commission to go to the coast of Africa on a slaving voyage. After pretending to trade there for some time, he suddenly bore away for the coast of America. He first fell in with the lesser Antilles Islands, beat up to Porto Rico and from thence to the small island of Mona, where he took in food and water. A storm spoiled the greater part of his bread and compelled him to put into St. Nicholas harbor, on the east side of Hispaniola, for a fresh supply; but the Spaniards refused to furnish him with more provisions. Sailing from thence he met with another storm, and it was with great difficulty that he reached Cape St. Anthony, on the west coast of Cuba. While lying there he mustered his officers and most of his crews, and addressed them thus:

"The time is now come that you should know the real object of this expedition as it was designed from the first. Nearly two years have passed since our countrymen who left France to make homes in Florida were set upon in the night and murdered by the most cruel and bloodthirsty creatures ever made in the image of God. First they fell upon the fort, where a feeble garrison had been left to protect the aged, the sick, the women and children. Like fiends they slew them in their beds, on their knees, or wherever found. No pity was shown, and even children of a tender age were slain. A few captives were reserved and subsequently hanged on a tree. The ships of John Ribault, a noble Frenchman, whom I knew, and whom, despite our differences in religion, I loved, were wrecked on the Florida coast, and a few days later he and his men fell into the power of Melendez. The Spaniards promised to spare them— nay, Melendez swore that if they would surrender they should all be sent to France. Believing the perfidious lies of the monster, our unfortunate ship- mates surrendered. They were immediately bound with cords and butchered in cold blood. These atrocities appeal to the heart of every patriotic Frenchman and call for vengeance. For two years the blood of our murdered kinsmen has cried out for vengeance, and, by the help of God, I will avenge them.

"There is more that appeals to my soul. Rumors have come that some of our people, escaping the general massacre, are living among the Indians in the forest. I was once rescued from drowning by a seaman named De Barre, of Dieppe, and was so grateful for his gallant preservation of my own life that I have ever since wished I might repay him. He perished in a riot; but his daughter, who went with Ribault to the New World, escaped the mas- sacre at Fort Carolinia, and there is a rumor that she lives in the forest among the Indians. We go to her rescue as well as to revenge."

He appealed to the humanity and patriotism of his followers, pointing out the inhuman cruelty of the Spaniards, until the Frenchmen were roused to a pitch of enthusiasm bordering on frenzy. At the end of his speech, he cried:

"How many of you demand vengeance?" A shout went up from the deck, in which every voice joined. "Vengeance!" was the cry.

Sailing through the straits of Bahama, he came upon the coast of Florida, where the Spaniards thought themselves so secure that they mistook the French ships for vessels from their own country, and saluted them accordingly. They were duly answered by De Gourges, who next night entered the river Tacatacouran, called by the French the Seine, fifteen miles from the river May or St. John.

"They will learn before long whom they have saluted," the fiery Gascon declared.

No wonder the Spaniards did not suspect that vengeance was at hand. The king of France had certainly winked at the extermination of the Huguenots, even if he had not sanctioned it. Protestantism, if not actually on the wane at this period, was at a stand-still, owing to the bitter persecutions, and no one dreamed of a single individual on his own account fitting out an expedition designed to deal out summary justice on the Spaniards.

By this time the Spaniards had rendered themselves odious to the natives, so that, mistaking De Gourges for a Spanish squadron, they prepared to oppose his landing. Suspecting their mistake, De Gourges sent his trumpeter, who had served under Laudonnière and understood their language, ashore.

The tribe which met them was that of Saturiova, with whom Francisco had left Hortense De Barre. The trumpeter, recognizing Saturiova before the boat touched the shore, called to him:

"Have no fear, my red brother, we are not Spaniards."

Recognizing them as French, Saturiova invited them to land and assured them of his hospitality. The trumpeter, who was master of their language, answered:

"We have come to renew our alliance with you, and will be friends of the Indians."

The old chief drew his mantle about his shoulders in his solemn, impressive manner and asked:

"Where is the chief of the boats?"

"He will come ashore in the morning."

"Saturiova will talk with him."

Returning to his vessel the trumpeter reported his interview with the chief.

"I will go and see this savage to-morrow," said De Gourges, "and if we can make an ally of him, he will prove invaluable to us."

Accordingly, next morning, with great pomp and ceremony to impress the Indians, De Gourges was rowed ashore, and advanced to meet the chief, who, surrounded by his principal warriors and advisers, stood on the shore to greet him.

"Saturiova is happy to greet white brothers from France once more," said the chief, "especially since the cruel men from Spain came, and killed many who were friends of the red men."

Carefully concealing the object of his visit, De Gourges casually asked:

"How are you getting along with the Spaniards?"

"Very badly," the chief answered. "They treat us cruelly and steal all they can. They are proud, and demand all our best furs and gold, and if we refuse they kill us."

"Are they really so bad?" asked De Gourges, as if hardly able to credit the story.

"They are worse—I hate them," and Saturiova struck the ground with his spear. "If the French will fight them, I will aid them with all my warriors."

De Gourges, not wishing to appear too anxious, seemed at first to hesitate, but finally answered:

"We came merely to pay you a friendly visit and renew the former league our people had with you. In fact we had no intention of war. If I found the Spaniards imposing on you, then I intended returning to France for a greater force to exterminate them; but since I have seen you and heard all you have said, I have changed my mind, and I am ready to aid you with my soldiers, ships, and guns."

The chief was so delighted that he embraced De Gourges in an ecstasy of joy. The French commandant continued: "Some of the Huguenots who fled from Fort Carolinia into the forest are said to be among your people. Do you know where any of them are?"

"I do."

"Can you bring them to me?"

"I have the pale lily given to me by the Spaniard who never came back."

"Why?"

"They say his countrymen imprisoned him."

"And you have the young French woman alive and well?"

"Yes."

"Bring all the French people you can find to me."

Saturiova assented and hurried away.

De Gourges sent a small scouting party into the woods, which, on their return, brought back a Spaniard and John Gyrot, whom they had captured. These two had gone out from Fort St. Mattheo to reconnoitre the strange fleet when they fell into the hands of the French.

No sooner was John Gyrot in the hands of his countrymen than his political and religious sentiments underwent a complete change. He guessed the reason for the visit of the French to Florida, and began to tremble for his own neck. No sooner was he taken to the presence of De Gourges than he declared himself a Frenchman escaping from the Spanish fort.

"I can hardly credit your story," said De Gourges.

"I was made a cruel slave by the Spaniards, monsieur," Gyrot declared. "I was making my escape to go and live with the Indians when I fell in with your people."

"Why is this Spaniard with you?" De Gourges asked.

Gyrot was momentarily confused before he could fix up a story to get out of this unforeseen difficulty; but he was not long at a loss for a lie that would do, and then he said:

"Having incurred the displeasure of an officer, he was sentenced to be shot, so he escaped with me." As the Spaniard knew no French he could not contradict the assertion.

"You may remain in camp," said De Gourges. "We expect others to-morrow who escaped from the massacre at Fort Carolinia, a young man and a young woman."

Gyrot started, and a gleam of joy flashed over his repulsive features. Who could the young woman be but Hortense De Barre? No other Huguenot was among the Indians. Gyrot's resolution was immediately formed. He began to relate the wrongs he had suffered at the hands of his Spanish masters, and most particularly did he describe one, Franciso Estevan, as a demon, whom he asked the privilege of killing with his own hand. Without deciding, De Gourges promised to give his request some thought. The French commandant was not altogether satisfied with Gyrot's stories, which in part failed to harmonize with accepted facts.

The Spaniard was sent on board a ship for safe-keeping, and while John Gyrot was given the privilege of the camp, a close watch was kept over him. Night passed and next morning Peter De Bray was brought in by some of the Indians, who announced that Saturiova and the white lily were coming. De Bray was overjoyed to meet with his countrymen; but was equally annoyed at finding John Gyrot among them. Before he could say a word to De Gourges, warning him of the treacherous rascal, the wily scoundrel seized De Bray's hand and began:

"My dear friend Peter, you know not how it gladdens my heart to see you again, and realize

that we are now among our own countrymen.
You, too, have suffered, my dear friend, but not
so much as I, who have been in prison and sick
and threatened with death. I saw my dearest
friends hanged before my very eyes and was powerless to render them aid," and here he tried to call
up a hypocritical tear, even going through the act
of brushing it away. "It was very sad, monsieur,
I assure you," he added.

"But—I heard you had not fared badly," began
De Bray.

"My dear friend, no one will ever know how
badly I did fare. I was reserved from death for a
greater torture by that fiend in human form, Francisco Estevan."

"Is he not a prisoner?"

"Temporarily, only temporarily," interrupted
John Gyrot. "You don't understand it, monsieur.
I will give you the particulars in due time, revealing all the cunning and devilish plans of Estevan,
and to your ears unfold a plot that would do credit
to the most cunning fiend of perdition." While
he still spoke in his hurried, excited manner, Saturiova approached with Hortense, who was clad in
the rich costume of an Indian princess. Their
moccasined feet made no noise and they joined the
group without Gyrot being aware of their presence.
He continued speaking hurriedly to forestall any-

thing De Bray might say derogatory to his own character.

"Monsieur De Gourges, if I were to tell you one-half of the cruelties perpetrated by Francisco Estevan, your blood would boil and your flesh would creep. He slew six of the Huguenots, flaying one alive, and my own back must bear the marks of his scourge, monsieur; but we will hang and quarter him, won't we, monsieur?"

"No," cried a sharp, silvery voice behind his back, sounding like the trump of doom in the ear of the guilty wretch. Wheeling about, he espied Hortense De Barre, her eyes flashing with indignation, her cheeks aflame, her lips parted, and her breast heaving. The dove had become an eagle, the lamb a tigress, and the meek girl an avenger. "Monsieur De Gourges, every word that base traitor utters is false. He betrayed Fort Carolinia to the Spaniards; he went secretly to their ships and laid the plans for the capture of the garrison; he gave the signal for the attack, and held the torch to light the Spaniards while they murdered his countrymen. He is a traitor, a libel on the very name of manhood, and his mission here is full of treason."

For a moment John Gyrot was stunned. He gazed at the beautiful girl, who in two worlds and under all the trying vicissitudes of life had defied him. He forgot his own peril, forgot everything save that after two years' fruitless search he was face to face with Hortense De Barre. With his dark, greenish eyes ablaze, and those sharp white teeth gnashing like the incisors of an enraged hedgehog, he looked at her, hissing:

"I have found you at last, now come with me!"

But there was one who had watched his movements, and, like a dark meteor, old Saturiova leaped between Gyrot and the girl, a long, keen knife in his hand.

"No!" he cried in his own tongue. "She is my daughter—touch her and die!"

Gyrot fell back, and, in the excitement which ensued, ran from the camp, and, with a defiant shout, leaped into the wood.

"He is gone to warn the Spaniards, monsieur," cried Hortense.

Before De Gourges could speak, Saturiova issued an order to four of his young men, and they plunged into the woods after the fugitive.

"TOUCH HER AND DIE!"

CHAPTER XVI.

THE incidents with which the foregoing chapter closed transpired so rapidly that De Gourges was stunned by the dénouement, as dramatic as it was unexpected, and could hardly comprehend the dangerous character of Gyrot until he had disappeared. Then, although four young Indians had been sent to bring back the fugitive, De Gourges still felt uneasy.

"We must capture or kill the scoundrel," the commandant declared. "I will send a party to arrest him."

"Your men know not the forest, nor are they accustomed to making long runs," said Saturiova. "They will be lost and perish in the wood. I have sent four swift young men to kill or seize him, and I will send fifty more to guard every path about the forts on this river, and also at St. Augustine, so that he can never reach the Spaniards."

"Do so at once."

Old Saturiova selected fifty of his young men,

16   241

sending twelve to watch each of the forts on May River, and fourteen to guard every avenue to St. Augustine. They were instructed to interfere with no one save the evil man with the face of death. They received their orders and all silently disappeared into the forest.

Peter De Bray assured De Gourges that nothing more could be done toward the capture of John Gyrot.

After the flight of the traitor, Hortense retired to the interior of the camp, and sat down on a log, her mind harassed with fears and doubts. If Gyrot reached St. Mattheo, Francisco would certainly be slain, for the Spaniards, incensed at the invasion of the French, would not spare one of their own countrymen who was friendly toward them. De Gourges went to her, and asked:

"Is this Mademoiselle De Barre?"

"It is, monsieur."

"I knew your father; he once saved my life, and I registered a vow that I would befriend him and his under any and all circumstances when in trouble. To fulfil that vow was one of the incentives which brought me here."

Hortense bowed her pretty head.

"Now, mademoiselle, tell me about yourself, your coming to America and your suffering here."

As briefly as she could, Hortense related her sad

story, especially that part which bore upon her emigration to America. She told of the incident at Beaucarre, her rescue of the Spanish student, the jealousy of Gyrot and his persistent persecutions. Finally she told of her emigration with Ribault in the last fleet to Florida and settling at Fort Carolinia, where, to her surprise, she met both Gyrot and Francisco Estevan. She told in detail the story of Gyrot's treachery to his countrymen, and the fidelity of Estevan. The awful carnage on that terrible night of September 21, 1565, was lived over again, and she dwelt particularly on the heroism of the young Spaniard, who had saved her and taken her to Saturiova. When the brave girl came to the picture of Francisco arrested and thrown into prison without the benefit of clergy, all for herself, she broke down and wept.

"Now, monsieur, I want to ask one favor before this attack is made," she said.

"What is it? If I can, I will grant it."

"I have learned that the priest Mendoza, who is a friend of Franciso Estevan, is unaware of his imprisonment. Let me go to Mendoza, plead his cause, and secure Francisco's release before you make the attack."

"Impossible, child; our plans would all be discovered and thwarted; but I will do all I can to save the prisoner."

"He will be slain in the attack, or put to death by his own people."

"Let us hope not. Cheer up, mademoiselle, and we will save him yet," said De Gourges on leaving her. But Hortense was far from being satisfied.

Meanwhile, Saturiova was not idle. On that same afternoon he summoned all the paraousties, or chiefs, who were either his allies or vassals, or over whom he had any control, and held a council of war with De Gourges and his officers. From the number of men each chief agreed to furnish, De Gourges found he would have quite a considerable army.

"It will be well to send scouts to the neighborhood of Fort Carolinia and ascertain its exact strength," suggested De Gourges. The plan was acquiesced in by Saturiova and he chose his nephew, Olacatora, to accompany any one whom the white chief might choose. Olacatora was an ambitious young brave, and felt a degree of pride at being selected for so important an office.

De Gourges chose a daring young Frenchman named D'Estampes. Before they departed the French commandant took D'Estampes aside and impressed on his mind the danger of his enterprise, and urged him to be cautious, vigilant, and brave. He assured him that the success of the enterprise and the lives of the soldiers depended on him. He enjoined on him the necessity of getting a correct report of the number of men and guns in the fort, to commit nothing to writing, but to retain everything in his mind. The scout promised to follow his instructions to the letter, and then the white man and Indian set out on their reconnoitring expedition.

While awaiting the return of the scouts, De Gourges was not idle. Having abandoned his original plan of attacking the fort by sea, he brought his arms and soldiers on shore. The soldiers were constantly kept busy training, and fighting mimic frays, that they might not forget how to handle the arquebus, sword, and halberd.

Hortense, refusing to go on shipboard, was assigned to the best tent De Gourges had in his camp, and received every attention possible from the generous commander, though he absolutely refused to permit her to make the mad pilgrimage to St. Augustine.

At the close of the third day D'Estampes and the Indian were seen returning, and word was at once sent to De Gourges, who was on board of his vessel. He came ashore and the chiefs assembled about the scouts to hear their report and lay plans for the future. D'Estampes said:

"The Spaniards have built two additional forts below Fort Carolinia, one on each side of the river.

All three of these forts are in good condition and
cannon are mounted on their works.   They are
garrisoned by four hundred men; but they live in
such perfect security that they can be very easily
surprised."

"Has   Gyrot   gained   the   forts?"   asked   De
Gourges.

"No, monsieur, we met one of the Indians sent
to capture him, and were informed that although
he had not been captured, he has been driven so
far up into the country and every avenue of escape
is so carefully guarded, that it will be impossible for
him to reach either of the forts or St. Augustine."

"From this report," said De Gourges, "it will
be seen that our only chance of success is by secrecy
and surprise."

He then held a long conference with Saturiova,
and they agreed upon a general rendezvous near the
Spanish forts, from whence they could march to
the attack.   When the conference was over, Hortense again appealed to the French commandant to
be permitted to make an effort for the release of
Francisco Estevan before the attack was made.
De Gourges declared that the thought was madness,
and assured her that he would do what he could
to save the young Spaniard, though he would not
consent to her mad desire, as it might jeopardize
all their plans.

She turned away in despair and was about to retire to her tent, when suddenly she met a tender gaze from a pair of great, dark eyes. It was the old chief's nephew, the brave young Olacatora.

This young man had for two years worshipped the white lily, or maiden of the sun, as she was sometimes called, at a distance. She was a being too great for him to approach in the light of a lover, and so strong was his affection that he asked nothing more than to be her slave. She had come to regard him as a devoted friend to whom she could intrust her life. At sight of the young warrior, a wild scheme for the release of Francisco, despite all De Gourges had said, suddenly entered her mind. She called Olacatora to her side and, speaking hurriedly in the Indian tongue, which she had mastered, said:'

"Olacatora, you have been my brother, will you help me now?"

"Olacatora will do the bidding of the maiden of the sun."

"The task is dangerous."

"He will do it or die."

There was no doubting those solemn words and earnest eyes. He meant all he said, and had she commanded him to leap off some towering summit to certain death below he would have done so.

"There is confined in the prison of Fort St.

Mattheo one who saved my life and took me to the good chief Saturiova, who was sentenced to dungeon and chains because he would not betray my hiding-place. John Gyrot, he with the evil face, has escaped and may reach the fort, despite the vigilance of the runners sent to stop him. There is in St. Augustine a priest who has power of life and death over prisoners, but who knows nothing of the imprisonment of his friend at St. Mattheo. While they lay their plans for the attack, come with me; we will go to St. Augustine, see Mendoza, and he will force Melendez to order the release of Francisco Estevan; then with the order we will hasten to St. Mattheo and set the prisoner free, before the arrival of the French."

Without betraying the slightest emotion at her request, the Indian answered:

"I will do it."

"It will soon be dark, Olacatora, and in an hour we will start. Meet me under the blasted pine on the hill."

No further planning was necessary. She knew the Indian would have everything needful for the journey at the rendezvous on time.

As soon as it was dark, Hortense stole from the tent and went to the spot. Standing by the old blasted pine, his arms folded across his breast, as motionless as the dead tree, was the young warrior.

Not a word was spoken when she joined him, and both started silently on their journey through the forest.

Two years among the red men had so inured Hortense to toil and hardship that the journey through the wilderness was not such an impossible affair as it might seem. All night long they travelled, with scarce a pause. At morning he built a fire and dressed a hare which he had slain and broiled it for their breakfast. While he was doing this, she slept upon the robe which he spread on the ground for her, and after breakfast they resumed their journey. The sky became overcast, the thunder rolled in the distance, and soon the rain began to fall, but they halted not. Francisco's life was at stake, and Hortense De Barre heeded not the toil and exposure. Her only thought was to see Mendoza and procure the pardon and release of the captive ere the blow was struck; for she feared it would be too late when the French reached St. Mattheo. On, over hill and dale, swamp and bayou, through drenching rain they pressed. Sometimes they came to swollen streams, which the Indian was forced to swim with the girl on his back.

A dark, stormy day was drawing to a close when Mendoza was informed that two Indians wished to see him. As Mendoza was quite enthusiastic over the conversion of the red people, he had them sent to his apartment, and was a little surprised to meet an Indian warrior and a young and pretty white woman in the costume of an Indian princess. Before he could recover from his amazement, the young woman said in Spanish:

"We have come, Father Mendoza, to inform you that a young Spaniard, a Catholic, has been for two years confined at St. Mattheo without the benefit of clergy, on the information of John Gyrot, an apostate Huguenot."

"There must be some mistake, my daughter. I have heard nothing of it."

"It is no mistake, father. Go ask Melendez and he will not deny it. This young Spaniard was studying to become a priest."

"A priest confined on the evidence of an apostate Huguenot! Melendez must be mad!"

"He was basely deceived by Gyrot."

"What is the priest's name?"

"Francisco Estevan."

Mendoza started to his feet and exclaimed:

"I know him in Spain, and he was a most devout Catholic. I supposed him in a monastery or convent in Cuba."

"He sailed for Cuba, and was captured by some French pirates, one of whom was John Gyrot, who has since maligned him to Melendez and procured his arrest and confinement in the darkest dungeon in St. Mattheo."

Mendoza was stunned at this intelligence. Could it be possible that Melendez, whose spiritual adviser he had been and whose confession he had received, had kept a prisoner for two years in a dungeon without his knowledge? The priest soon formed his resolution.

"I will go and confront Melendez with this, and if he has been guilty he shall sign Estevan's pardon and issue an order for his immediate release."

"Will you bring the order to me?" asked Hortense, breathing a silent prayer for strength. The priest, moved by her earnestness, answered:

"I will."

Mendoza could be fiery and eloquent as well as terrible when roused. At thought of one of his religious order being convicted on the evidence of an apostate heretic, at the knowledge of one of the best Spanish families calumnied by Gyrot, his blood boiled and he burst in on Melendez with the fury of a hurricane, making that fanatic tremble in his seat. He upbraided him for lack of confidence in the Church, and accused him of being blinded by Gyrot, whose tool he had been. In vain Melendez tried to explain his compact with Gyrot, by which the successful attack on Fort Carolinia had been made, and told him of the oath he had made. It was without avail. The priest could dissolve all compacts and grant absolution from all oaths. Nothing but a pardon and order for the release of Francisco would answer. Overwhelmed by the fury of the priest, Melendez hastened to grant the pardon and sign the order for his release. The priest returned with the latter, which he gave to Hortense, whom he found waiting, and, without halting for refreshments or rest, she set out for St. Mattheo.

"We have not a moment to lose, Olacatora," she said, as they hurried along. "My footsteps grow heavy, and I fear I shall faint. Should I fall by the way, you must not wait for me, but take the free-paper and run to Fort St. Mattheo and give it to the governor of the fort."

The Indian assented by the usual grunt characteristic of his race. They pressed on through rain and sunshine, daylight and darkness, over hill and dell, through swamps, across streams and places deemed almost impassable, pausing only a few moments at a time. The girl made no complaint and journeyed on in silence. She who had been so tenderly reared in a home of ease and luxury was now a heroine, enduring what might overcome a man. Once they caught a glimpse of a white-faced fugitive, flying through the wood, pursued by three young Indians, who were driving him farther away into the forest. He saw her not, but Hortense recognized that evil-eyed man and thought, "God's vengeance is falling on him with a heavy hand."

On to Fort St. Mattheo pressed the fair Huguenot and her companion, muddy, wet, and hungry.

"God grant I may be in time!" she prayed.

They had travelled all night, and her strength was nearly exhausted, when, at early dawn, before her blurred vision rose the ramparts of St. Mattheo, with the spire of the small chapel, reared on the blood-stained soil of her slaughtered countrymen. She was faint and dizzy, and so exhausted that she tottered as she walked, but with a superhuman effort she threw off her increasing weakness and cried:

"No, no! I must not faint now! I must not faint now!"

.   .   .   .

At the appointed hour De Gourges with his troops was at the place of rendezvous. Here he met Saturiova and his chiefs, who were very punctual. The place of rendezvous was on the banks of the River Somme, called by the savages "Suraba." When they had assembled, De Gourges said to the chiefs:

"I want to exact from you a solemn promise that, as you have led us into this quarrel, you will not desert us."

"My white brother need have no fears," answered Saturiova. "I am here with my warriors; my friends are here with their warriors; we are all ready to go with the thunder-makers and exterminate the Spaniards."

"Are you willing to go where I shall direct and do what I shall command?" asked De Gourges. A grunt of assent was the response.

It being quite late, the army encamped, intending to begin the final march in the morning.

CHAPTER XVII.

SOON after dark a heavy rain set in and continued all night, accompanied by a high wind, thunder, and lightning. By morning the streams were swollen, the low lands inundated, and the expedition was in serious danger of an utter failure.

De Gourges began to grow discouraged when it was reported that the road by which they were going to make the attack was impassable. Was there no other way by which the fort could be reached? Perhaps the Indians knew of some other route. De Bray found a young brave who agreed to guide them to the fort. All day and night the rain continued to fall, but by noon the next day it cleared a little. De Gourges drew his men up once more for the final march, and said:

"I want to remind every Frenchman that the hour to strike has come. Remember that for two years your slaughtered countrymen have slept unavenged in nameless graves. Let no man falter. Come on."

255

Led by the guide, the army began their march. Heavy armor was generally discarded at this day, being ineffective against bullets and interfering with celerity of movement, though helmet and breast-plate were still worn to protect the head and breast. Night came, and after a short halt to rest the march was continued. The sky was clear and the new moon, like a horn of silver, hung in the sky, while one by one the stars opened their bright little eyes to watch the silent army. During the remainder of the night only short halts were made, when the guide, momentarily at fault, sought a new course. All night he led them by a safe but roundabout route, and just before dawn of day announced that on crossing a stream before them they would be in full view of one of the forts.

"Is the stream deep?" De Gourges asked.

The Indian signified the depth by pointing to his breast.

"Then we will wade it."

De Gourges ordered his men to fasten their powder-flasks on their helmets and to carry their swords and guns in their hands. Day had already begun to dawn, and the shadows in the forest grew momentarily lighter, revealing the pale, stern faces of the soldiers and officers. The Indian guide first plunged into the stream, De Gourges following. Then the whole army entered the water, which, in places, came quite up to their armpits. De Gourges, gaining the opposite bank, turned about and cautioned his men against making any noise.

All were safely over at last, and the soldiers were allowed to stand a few moments while the water ran from their soaked garments. From this point De Gourges determined to reconnoitre the fort in person, and, with D'Estampes, De Bray, and Saturiova, he set out through the brushwood and tall grass. They moved with the utmost caution, and shortly after sunrise were rewarded by gaining a point from whence they had a view of the doomed fort. De Gourges was a little startled by seeing the people inside the fort in motion as if excited over something, and feared that John Gyrot had eluded his Indian pursuers, reached the fort, and spread the alarm.

It afterward appeared that the cause of the commotion was the rumor that two Indians had at dawn reached St. Mattheo with an order for the release of a prisoner. This caused the people to gather in groups and discuss who the prisoner could be. A great many of the men were also busy repairing a fountain. De Gourges waited until the flurry seemed to partially subside, and went back to his men. The Indians had kept their secret well, and John Gyrot, though not captured, had not been permitted to reach any of the Spanish settle-

17

ments, so to this very moment the Spaniards were wholly unaware of the presence of the French in Florida.

De Gourges divided his little army into two parties, taking command of the first division himself and giving the second to his brave lieutenant, Cassenove, whom he sent to attack from the right flank, while he advanced in front, leaving the Indians to fight in their own way.

It was a lovely morning; the storm seemed over instead of about to begin. Never is Florida more like an earthly paradise than in the month of May, when rare exotics seem to burden the air with their perfume and the carols of tropical songsters fill the woods with melody. No wonder Ponce de Leon thought he had found the land where men never die, for among the green savannahs, orange-groves, and palms of Florida nature is always young.

The Spaniards in the fort on this sunny morning little dreamed that just beyond the gentle swell of ground on the north, hidden by tall grass and shrubs and the blooming roses, whose sullen fires seemed half quenched in the dew, ranks of armed men were advancing upon the fort. All along the line of Frenchmen there rose little clouds of pale blue smoke from the lighted match-cords.

" Forward!"

Low and stern was the voice.

De Gourges himself took the lead and guided them over the hill. When the fort was in sight of the attacking party, at a word from their leader they trailed their arms and dashed at it.

Three persons were seen coming from the direction of Fort St. Mattheo. One was an Indian, one a young man whose white face and mouldy clothing told a sad story of long confinement, and the third a white girl in the faded and worn garb of an Indian princess.

No one was visible at the fort save an engineer who had mounted the platform and stood near a pair of culverins, watching the party coming from St. Mattheo, and wondering what strange power the Indian maiden had brought to bear on Melendez to procure the liberation of the prisoner at St. Mattheo. Then he turned his gaze northward and was amazed to see that long line of men coming out of the woods with guns and matchlocks in their hands, and stooping as they ran. With a cry of surprise, he fired the culverins and shouted:

"The French! the French! To arms! to arms!"

For the first time that long line of advancing Frenchmen broke the silence with a howl of rage; then the tall savage who walked behind Hortense and the rescued Spaniard ran with the fleetness of a deer to the fort, leaped upon the platform, and, seizing a lance which lay near the culverins, drove it through the engineer's body, laying him dead at his feet.

" Retribution! " shouted De Gourges in trumpet tones, leaping on the ramparts and waving his sword in the air.

" The French! The Huguenots! " groaned the panic-stricken Spaniards. The army came down and poured a galling fire .into the Spaniards, mowing them down under the withering hail of death, and then with drawn swords they leaped on those whom their bullets had spared, cutting them down right and left. No prayer for mercy could avail. When a Spaniard begged his life on his knees, he was answered:

" You spared not Ribault and his people," and was run through.

It was not the retribution of God, but of man, that fell on those Spaniards, some of whom were innocent, having come from Spain since the terrible event at Fort Carolinia. They made little resistance, but fled pell-mell over the works, running toward the woods right into the ranks of the second division under Cassenove. Being put between two fires the entire garrison of sixty were cut down, save a few who were reserved for hanging, according to the plan of De Gourges.

So absorbed were Hortense and Estevan over the

"RETRIBUTION!" SHOUTED DE GOURGES IN TRUMPET TONES.

latter's recent escape from prison, that they saw not the advancing army of De Gourges until the sharp crack of the engineer's culverins roused them to a sense of their danger, and, looking up, they saw the armed hosts of De Gourges advancing.

"Come, Francisco, we must fly!" she cried, seizing his hand.

Fatigue was forgotten and all her energy returned. The French were on the fort, and with no other thought than preserving the life of him whom she had rescued, she held his hand tightly clasped in her own, and ran to meet the advancing army.

Half a score of swords were shortened, and De Gourges, not recognizing Hortense at first glance, cried:

"Cut them down! Allow none to escape!"

"Spare him! he saved me!" groaned Hortense.

"Hortense De Barre!" gasped De Gourges. "You here! I commanded you not to leave camp."

"This is Estevan who rescued me. Spare him!" she answered.

"Let them pass to the rear."

The ranks parted, and they passed through. The French dashed on to vengeance, and Hortense led Estevan over the hill out of sight of the scene of carnage; then she sank exhausted on the ground.

Francisco Estevan kneeled at her side, support-

ing the head of the half-fainting girl, while the
roar of battle across the hill grew louder every moment. The boom of artillery from the second fort
joined in with the din of carnage, and awoke the
sleeping echoes for many miles around. Estevan
heeded not the sounds of conflict. He saw only the
sad, sweet face of his half-unconscious preserver, on
which rested a smile of triumph. He heard only
the low, faint whisper:

"I saved him, I saved him!"

His long imprisonment had wrought great changes
in Francisco. He had learned that man's fanaticism was no evidence of God's love. For two·
years his mind had been blinded to earthly objects
that he might look within and see spiritual things,
and he was a wiser and better man than before.

Hortense and the Indian had arrived at early
dawn at Fort St. Mattheo, and presented the order
to the governor of the fort for the release of the
prisoner. The governor could hardly believe at first
that Melendez would issue such an order; but the
writing was unmistakably the admiral's, and he
had the prisoner brought up, and notified him that
he was free. Hortense, whom he could scarcely
recognize in her Indian costume, came and took
his hand, and hurried him away so that the bewildered Spaniard could hardly comprehend how it
all had come about. Estevan was led out into the

open air; he felt the sweet-scented breezes, and
saw the glorious sunshine of morning, and then,
before a word of explanation could be given, they
were rushing hand in hand through charging armies
and all about them was death and carnage. In
fact, he was hardly sure that it was not all a dream,
from which he would awake to find himself again
in his loathsome dungeon. The sun was so bright
it almost blinded him. The forest was greener,
and the wild flowers of vermillion and gold sweeter,
and the soft southern skies bluer than he had ever
seen them before.

The thundering jars of war over the hill alone
reminded him that it was all a stern reality. He
had scarcely spoken since his liberation; no explanation had been made to him, and he could not
understand why Hortense was lying there, pale
and exhausted, her beautiful Indian costume stained
with mud and travel. As yet the half-fainting
girl could only murmur:

"I have saved him; yes, thank God, I have
saved him!"

"Hortense!" he said at last, and started at the
sound of his own voice.

"Francisco!"

"How did it come about? Am I free?"

"Yes."

"What means that carnage over the hill?"

"The French have come to destroy the Spaniards."

Both were silent for awhile, and then she was able to sit up and gaze about her. By slow degrees the rescued man came to realize that it was no dream, and that he was in truth and in fact liberated. He had passed two miserable years in the dungeon, and there had been a great conflict waging within his breast, and at times his wrongs had seemed to cry out to heaven for vengeance. When he had finally despaired of freedom he was suddenly and mysteriously liberated. No wonder that he was filled with amazement and hardly able to believe it a reality.

"Where have you been, Hortense?" he asked, when he found her strong enough to converse a little. "What has been your fate since we parted on that morning so long ago?"

She briefly recounted her last two years' experience with the Indians, who had treated her with kindness and respect. Saturiova had been a father to her, and had sheltered and protected her. Then Estevan wanted to know all about the French army coming to Florida and his own liberation.

Hortense had grown a little stronger, and she told him of the arrival of De Gourges and his designs against the Spanish. Having learned that Mendoza was ignorant of his imprisonment, and as drowning people grasp at straws, she determined to appeal to the priest to save him. Her flight from the French camp with Olacatora and their terrible journey were depicted in as few words as possible. Then she told of the success of the expedition and the return, and concluded with:

"And, with God's help, I saved you."

They were a long time silent. She had reduced her strength by the exertion of talking, and for several moments Estevan was too much overcome to speak. At last he mastered his emotions sufficiently to say:

"Again you have saved my life, and such obligations am I under to you that if I could die for you I would be happy."

"Let us not talk of death nor of ourselves. Just across the hill, God's creatures are being slaughtered like sheep."

"Is it not retribution?"

"God says, 'Thou shalt not kill.'"

"Would you spare those whom your country men slay?"

"I would."

"Yet they slew your relatives and friends and drove you to a life of exile among the savages."

"May God forgive them!"

The Christianity of forgiveness, mercy, love, and kindness was little known and less practised during the age of bigotry; and he, who from infancy had been set apart for God's work, was amazed to find a real forgiving spirit among mortals. He thought there must be something wrong, either with her or with himself, and, after a few moments' silence, he asked:

"Can you, a Protestant, forgive a Catholic?"

"What matters it if one is Protestant or Catholic? Are we not all God's creatures?"

"But some choose to believe Him, and some do not."

"All believe in God. There is only a difference in the mode of worship. Should I slay my brother because he differs from me about the mode of worshipping the same Supreme Being? God forgive the people for their short-sightedness, and may they all see His holy way without dimming the path to glory with blood and crime."

They might be in danger in their present position, he thought, and he asked her if she was able to go on. She said she could walk again, and, leaning on his arm, they wandered into the forest, neither knowing which way they went. They crossed a creek on a log and hurried on into the wilderness, going farther and farther from those sounds of conflict.

Francisco Estevan's mind was busy with the

past, the present, and the future. What were they to do? Should the French prevail would she be strong enough to protect him against their vengeance, and should his own countrymen succeed, would Hortense be spared? Their condition was deplorable. They dared not trust to either Frenchmen or Spaniards, and John Gyrot, their archenemy, was in the forest. Their plans were sudden, and formed more on the impulse of the moment than from reason.

In their wanderings they left the sound of battle farther and farther in the distance, until even the roar of cannon died away. At last they came to the mossy banks of a brooklet, and, knowing how tired his fair companion must be, he said:

"Let us rest awhile."

They sat down, and, after a long and thoughtful silence, the young ecclesiastic asked:

"Hortense, you are a Protestant and have suffered by the persecutions of the Catholics; do you believe there will be any Papists in heaven?"

"Yes; all good Papists will go there."

"Then you think there are good Catholics?"

"There are many, and God will bless them."

"Will there be fellowship between Catholics and Protestants in heaven?"

"In heaven the scales of superstition and the

motes of bigotry will be removed from our eyes, and we shall see each other as we really are. All will be brothers there."

"And will they be brothers here?"

"Yes, when the age of ignorance and superstitious bigotry gives place to reason, then the good Catholic and good Protestant will clasp hands across the smouldering fires of martyrdom, and all will worship God as different members of one great family."

He was silent for a moment, and then broke forth with:

"You are not only the best, but the wisest person living."

At this moment a small party of Spaniards, who had broken through the ranks of their enemies, were seen flying through the wood toward them. Francisco and Hortense had just time to conceal themselves, when the frightened Spaniards rushed by. One of them dropped his sword, but was either too much frightened to miss it or to pause to pick it up. When they were gone, Hortense said:

"Secure the sword; we may need it."

He did so.

CHAPTER XVIII.

NOT AS SPANIARDS AND MARINERS, BUT AS TRAI-
TORS, ROBBERS, AND MURDERERS.

THE fugitives, realizing that they were not safe
in their present location, continued to retreat, but
were compelled to travel slowly, owing to the exhausted condition of Hortense. Her feet were becoming sore from frequent bruises and long travel,
and her moccasins were so worn as to form little
protection. The future to them was a dark blank
into which they could not project a single plan.
For the present they insinctively resolved to keep
out of the hands of both the French and Spanish,
and see how affairs would turn out. Their food
was the wild fruit which grew in abundance.

When night came he cut some branches with his
sword and made her a bed of leaves, on which she
slept as peacefully and sweetly as if at home. The
young Spaniard kept guard, watching the stars
which he had not seen for so many months. He
found liberty and pure air so sweet that he had no
inclination to sleep. Several times during the
night escaped fugitives could be heard hurrying

through the wood, recalling that horrible night at
Carolinia, when the Huguenots were slain, and he
thought:

"Perhaps, after all, it is justice."

When morning dawned he killed a bird with a
stone, and dressing it, broiled it over the smouldering embers of a camp-fire left by the French
army.   He gave the cooked bird to Hortense, who
insisted on his sharing it with her.

As they journeyed still farther into the forest
he tried to form some plan for the future, but was
unable as yet to come to any definite conclusion.
To wait, hope, and depend on circumstances to help
them out seemed their only choice.   They were
walking slowly and painfully along the forest path
when they espied a man coming toward them.
One glance at the white face, stooped shoulders,
and cruel eyes, and despite the changes wrought by
hunger, toil, and exposure, Hortense De Barre
recognized John Gyrot.

He had managed to shake off his pursuers, and
was on his way to Fort St. Mattheo, when he met
a wounded Spaniard, a fugitive from the massacre.   He gave Gyrot a sword and told him of
the attack on the forts.   Gyrot abandoned the
wounded Spaniard, and was on his way to St. Augustine, when he came upon Francisco and Hortense.

"Monsieur and mademoiselle, a delightful morning," said Gyrot. Days of flight and hardship had not robbed his white face of the ironical sneer which had become habitual.

Hortense recoiled as she would from a loathsome serpent, and Gyrot, observing her aversion, advanced a step or two nearer, and continued:

"I have longed to find mademoiselle, and now that I have, I shall return with her in triumph to St. Augustine."

"Stop!" cried Estevan, seizing his sword in his right hand. "Señor Gyrot, advance another step at your peril."

"Oh! the prisoner has escaped; the priest has become a soldier. Back to your cage, you dangerous beast, or I may in truth punish you!"

Without paying any heed to his insulting remark, Francisco Estevan added:

"Advance another step toward the señorita and I will run you through the body."

"Monsieur's words are strong; but I doubt if he hath the courage of which he boasts."

"John Gyrot, if you go your way I will not harm you; if you remain, one of us must die."

"Very well, we will see if a priest can handle a sword."

The Frenchman drew his own blade and carelessly threw away the scabbard.

"O God, they are going to fight!" Hortense groaned, her face pale with dread and her eyes dimmed with tears.

"Get out of the way, Hortense," Estevan whispered, "and pray to God for victory."

She ran and fell upon her knees behind a tree, where, burying her face in her hands, she prayed. The combatants spoke not, but soon she heard the clash of steel against steel, and their heavy breathing told her how fierce was the conflict. She dared not look up lest her eyes might behold that which would have driven her mad. The combat seemed to the anxious girl to last for hours. A curse of rage from John Gyrot made her hope that he was getting worsted. The blows fell thicker and faster, and the fight had reached its zenith, when there came a sharp, wild cry, a groan and then a fall.

It was over, but how had it ended? She would have given worlds to know, yet she dared not look up to see. Some one was approaching, and yet she had not the courage to glance up and see whether it was a friend or foe. A hand touched her, and a voice which she recognized as Estevan's said:

"It is all over—let us go."

With a sob of joy she started to her feet and asked:

"Are you wounded?"

"Not a scratch."

He led her in another direction, that she might not be horrified by that ghastly object lying among the bushes, staining the grass to crimson with its life-blood.

. . . .

For the present it will be necessary to take leave of Francisco and Hortense, and return to De Gourges and his army, whom we left just after the storming of the first fort.

No sooner had the Spaniards been driven from the first fort than their friends in the second began an incessant fire on the French

"IT WAS OVER, BUT HOW HAD IT ENDED?"

with their cannon; but De Gourges drew out the artillery from the first fort, and played on the Spaniards so effectually, while the Indians aided him so vigorously, that the enemy deserted the fort and betook themselves to the woods, where all were captured or slain save a few who managed to make their escape.

18

The main fort, Carolinia, or St. Mattheo, still
remained to be reduced.   It being the strongest of
the three, De Gourges hesitated about attacking it
at once.   The entire day had been spent in reduc-
ing the first two, and his men were considerably
exhausted, especially as they had marched nearly
all the preceding night.

"We must wait and rest," he said to Lieutenant
Cassenove, who was eager to dash on St. Mattheo
and make an end of the business.   "The soldiers
and Indians," continued De Gourges, "are too
much fatigued.   We need food, rest, and sleep;
besides, we must learn something of the fort we are
to attack."

"How will you?"

"Have we no prisoners?"

"Yes, several."

"Bring one to me."

Cassenove left the commandant and soon returned
with an old Spanish sergeant.

"Do you speak French?" asked De Gourges.

The Spaniard shook his head.   De Gourges had
some knowledge of the Spanish, gained while a
slave at the galleys, and in that language proceeded
to interrogate him in regard to the fort.

The old sergeant shook his head and answered:
"I cannot betray my countrymen."

"You must answer my questions, or I will hang you."

The sergeant proved a little stubborn, and De Gourges sent for a rope and had a noose fixed over his neck. When thus confronted with death, the sergeant proceeded to give him information regarding the fort.

"Have you told me the truth?" asked the French commandant.

"Yes."

Producing a crucifix, De Gourges made him swear to the truth of his statement. The French commandant realized that he had no means of succeeding against the remaining fort, save by a scalade. The two following days were passed in making ladders and preparing to scale the fort. In the mean while, De Gourges planted such a number of Indians around the fort that it was impossible for the Spaniards to escape or come to any knowledge of his strength.

The Spanish commandant, who was enterprising as well as bold, caused one of his men to disguise himself like an Indian and mingle with the besiegers, who, having thrown up breastworks and planted cannon, occasionally bombarded the fort. The cannon were small and the fort strong, so the chances of a breech were not very great. At night

Olacatora sought out the French commander and informed him that they had a spy from the fort in their midst. De Gourges was not a little amazed at the information and asked who he was.

"A Spaniard from the fort, disguised as an Indian. Shall I slay him?"

De Gourges, thinking he might use the spy to a good advantage, answered:

"By no means; but take with you four of your strongest men, seize him from behind, bind him, and bring him to me."

The Indian bowed and silently retired. In an hour they returned with the spy bound. De Gourges gazed at the man, who met his gaze with faltering eye.

"You came to our camp to spy. Do you know what the fate of a spy is?"

The Spaniard began to implore him to spare his life. Although De Gourges at first designed him for the gallows, he concluded that he might use him to a better purpose, and he spared him on condition that he give a faithful description of the fort, and all the information he knew concerning the Spaniards. The fellow freely told all he knew, and agreed to go and show them the way to the fort, and, in fact, a great part of De Gourges' success was owing to the information this man communicated.

The night before the final attack on the fort, De Gourges sent for Olacatora. The Indian came and the commandant said:

"I want an explanation, Olacatora, for your strange disappearance, also the disappearance of Hortense De Barre, and how we found you here."

The Indian hesitated for a few moments, and then told the story of their journey to St. Augustine, its object, and the rescue of the prisoner at St. Mattheo. At first the French commandant was inclined to feel angry at the girl who had defied his authority; but reflection cooled his anger, for she had acted a noble, self-sacrificing part.

"Have you seen them since the attack?" he asked.

"No."

"They must be lingering in the wood."

"Yes."

"We will find them as soon as we have humbled Fort Carolinia, and I will bring Hortense home with me."

The sigh that escaped the Indian's lips was not unnoticed by the French commandant.

"Poor fellow, can he not see that the man whom he rescued is his rival?" thought De Gourges, when the Indian was gone.

Next morning everything was ready for the attack. De Gourges made such disposition of the

Indians as would render it extremely difficult for any of the Spaniards to escape when the fort should be taken. Under direction of the sergeant and spy he advanced to the attack, marching to the top of a little hill, from whence he had a full view of the strength and weakness of the fort. It was his intention to make a demonstration and delay the attack until 'next morning; but scarce had he reached the hill when he discovered a commotion within the fort.

"What does that mean?" asked De Gourges.

"They are going to make a sortie and attack us," answered Cassenove, who saw a body of men headed by fourteen musketeers pass through the gate and advance up the hill. "Monsieur, there comes the flower of the Spanish army."

"I see, and we shall prepare a trap for them."

De Gourges quickly wheeled his men and placed the divisions so as to flank the enemy and cut off all possible chance of retreat. The French had their match-cords lighted and gun-pans open to receive the Spaniards. The wheel-lock pistols had just come into use, and De Gourges was armed with a pair of those weapons. Taking the spanner from his belt he wound up the mechanism of the locks as the enemy advanced and waited on the hill to send death into their ranks, while his main lines were concealed behind some low bushes and grass.

On came the enemy directly toward the hillock
on which De Gourges stood, a pistol in each hand.
When within musket range they fired and charged
the French. The concealed lines now rose and
poured in a volley front and flank, which mowed
down the gallant Spaniards. Their leader saw
that the situation was desperate, but not once did
he think of returning. He sounded the old Spanish war-cry which had cheered Balboa, Cortez, and
Pizarro to deeds of valor, but it failed to bring
victory. They did not battle with heathen, but
with an enraged civilized foe. Matchlocks were
thrown aside, and with swords, lances, and halberds
they flew at each other. De Gourges, having
emptied his pistols, drew his sword and plunged
into the thickest of the fray. The Spanish
leader was slain, but his companions fought des-
perately until one by one they fell to rise no more.

This slaughter being made under the eyes of the
besieged, they lost all heart, and, regardless of the
orders of officers, who realized that their only hope
lay in defending the fort, they leaped over the
works and ran away like frightened sheep into the
woods. Here a terrible fate awaited them. Saturiova, who was itching to get at the enemy, and
who began to fear that the French would have all
the glory to themselves, saw, with no little degree
of satisfaction, the enemy rushing right into his

hands.　A yell, as if ten thousand demons had suddenly broken lose, rose on the air, and the Indians fell on them right and left, front and rear; wherever they turned they were met by merciless enemies, who beat them down with clubs, pierced them with javelins, or shot them with arrows. The Spaniards endeavored to escape another way, but were met by De Gourges, who laid most of them dead on the spot.　To complete his revenge, he saved the rest from the hands of the savages that he might resign them to those of the executioner.　De Gourges then ordered all the captives to be taken to the large oak on which so many Frenchmen had perished, and when he had ranged them beneath it he said:

"This punishment is but a just retribution. Two years ago you found a handful of Frenchmen, women and children, in that fort, who had come to the wilderness seeking homes.　You fell on them and cruelly murdered them, and on this very tree on which I intend to hang you, you hanged all whom you had not slain."

One of the Spaniards interposed that he had nothing to do with the massacre, as he had come to Florida subsequently to the event; but De Gourges answered that his nation had done it, and his presence sanctioned the deed, so he must die with the others.　Every one was hanged upon the tree, on which De Gourges placed the following inscription in imitation of Melendez:

"*I do not hang these people as Spaniards, nor as the spawn of infidels, but as traitors, robbers, and murderers.*"

The detestable example of Melendez was not sufficient excuse for such horrible retaliation, especially when we consider that most of the guilty escaped, and nearly all on whom the wrath of De Gourges was visited were innocent of the blood of the Huguenots. De Gourges was no more than a pirate, for he was not legally entitled to sail on the coast of Florida, much less to make such reprisals; but in those days the morals of nations and individuals were lax. Spain had acquired immense treasures in the New World, had grown powerful in conquest, and was an object of envy for every European power. Envy is the brother of hate, and piracies against the wealthy Spaniards were considered legitimate enterprises, and many European powers applauded the work of the Frenchmen. It must be acknowledged, however, that De Gourges undertook this expedition from very disinterested motives; for before he entered upon it he knew that he had neither men to keep the forts nor money to pay them, and that it was impossible to procure them subsistence even for money.

Satisfied with having avenged his slaughtered

countrymen, De Gourges demolished the three
forts, placed their artillery on board his own vessels, and prepared to return to Europe. Saturiova
urged the French to remain and hold Florida,
promising him the aid of all his warriors, but De
Gourges knew the Indians would be insufficient
against the horde of Spaniards who would be sent
against them. The savages loaded the French
with the most extravagant praises for an action
which was so much in their own manner, but
which far exceeded their abilities to perform.
Search was made for Hortense, but she could not
be found, and as the French were fearful lest a
heavy re-enforcement might come from St. Augustine, they set sail on the third of May, and on the
sixth of June arrived at Rochelle, having suffered
greatly on the voyage from storms and famine.

Before their return, the court of Spain, having
received intelligence of the expedition, fitted out a
squadron to intercept De Gourges, from which he
narrowly escaped. Upon landing, his old friend,
the Marshal De Moutluc, highly extolled his valor
and conduct, and advised him to go to court.

Fortunately for De Gourges, at this moment the
Protestant party was so powerful in France that
the government dared not provoke it by inflicting
on him any unreasonable severity, and the French
in general, Catholic as well as Protestant, approved

what he had done. On the other hand, the friendship of Spain happened at this time to be necessary
to the French king and the Catholic part of his
government. De Gourges was coldly received at
the French court, and was secretly warned to with-
draw to avoid the fury of the queen-mother, Catharine de Medici, and the Spaniard faction, who
pressed the king to have De Gourges arrested and
sent to Madrid to be tried for piracy.

The avenger of the Huguenots fled to Rouen,
where he was concealed by the president, De
Marigny, and so reduced were his circumstances
that he owed his daily life to that magistrate's
generosity. This persecution only tended to increase his fame, however, which at last made such
an impression on the French king that he restored
him to favor. It is said by some that Queen
Elizabeth offered him a place in her navy, which he
declined. Don Antonio of Portugal offered him
command of a fleet he was fitting out to recover
the crown of Portugal from PHILIP II. of Spain;
but while De Gourges was going to take possession
of that honorable commission, he suddenly fell sick,
and after a short illness died at Tours.

CHAPTER XIX.

THE morning after the fatal encounter with Gyrot, Francisco Estevan received so much evidence of the success of De Gourges' attack on the forts that he resolved to return to the French with the girl, who was growing more lame every mile they travelled. He asked Hortense if she would not like to go to her people.

"I would," she answered.

She bore up with wonderful fortitude, and had scarcely uttered a murmur, though she suffered continually.

"Do you think the French will march to St. Augustine?" he asked.

"I do not know."

"I would take you there, but we might only be running into another scene of carnage and danger, of which we have already had enough, so we had better go to the French fleet."

"I think so," she answered.

Hortense was too weak to travel rapidly. Her

feet were sore and her moccasins so worn as to afford but little protection. That evening they met some Indians, who told them of the fall of St. Mattheo and the retreat of the French to their ships. One of the Indians belonged to Saturiova and he gave Francisco a javelin, a bow, some arrows, and, what was of more value, some food.

When the Indians were gone, Francisco said:

"Hortense, we must hasten or the French will embark before we overtake them."

She made no answer and they journeyed on in silence. At every mile they met parties of Indians returning from the war, and from them received a full account of the destruction of the forts and the utter annihilation of the Spaniards. From one of the Indians Francisco procured a pair of moccasins for Hortense, whose feet were almost bare. They met a part of Saturiova's warriors, who told them that their chief, with many of his men, had gone to see the French embark and give them their parting blessing.

Despite all his energy and anxiety, with Hortense so lame, Francisco was only able to make three or four miles a day, while the French army was no doubt travelling much faster.

Next morning he came upon two Indians with whom he had been acquainted before his imprisonment, and prevailed on them to make a sort of a litter of two poles with a seat of bark between, on which he placed Hortense. The litter was carried between the two stout Indians, and they went so much faster that he began to hope they would reach the French fleet before it sailed.

One evening, when but a few miles from the river, the Indians came to an abrupt halt, put down the litter, and began to make preparations for camping.

"Won't you go on?" Francisco asked. "We are but three or four hours' journey from the fleet." The oldest of the Indians shook his head and said:

"No."

"But the ships may sail before we can reach them in the morning," urged Francisco.

"Indians are tired, and will not go until morning."

"Morning may be too late. The señorita's people will leave, and she will be left behind. She has been a long while from home."

Francisco Estevan, from what he had heard of the French expedition, had come to the conclusion that De Gourges had only come to strike a blow and retreat. The French had no intention of attempting to found a permanent colony in Florida. Since the French did not attack St. Augustine, he surmised they were not strong enough.

They had good cause to dread Melendez and would
not linger long in the country, so the young Spaniard knew that every moment was precious, and he
urged upon the Indians the necessity of reaching the
river that night. No one save those acquainted
with the American aborigines can appreciate Indian
obstinacy. He is sullen and stubborn, refusing
to be moved by threats, though susceptible to
bribery, and had Francisco possessed a few trinkets
he might have hired the savages to make some extra exertions. As he had just escaped from prison
and had nothing to excite their cupidity, all he
could do was to await their pleasure.

"I have done all I can," he said somewhat
despairingly. "I have nothing to give them, and
I cannot force them to go on."

"You have done what you could; think no more
about it," the brave girl answered. She made no
complaint, not even uttering a sigh of regret.

"But to be so near the ships and know the danger of their sailing is maddening."

"If they sail my condition will be no worse than
before," she answered, her face full of hope and
trust.

"No, I trust it will be better," he answered.

"Then let us not complain," said the patient Hortense, while there flitted over her face a sweet smile.
"If God wills it otherwise, His will be done."

"It is on your account alone that I regret it," he returned with a sigh. "I have no intention of going to France, but the disappointment to you will be overwhelming. If you could only walk a little we might reach it."

"My feet forbid my walking a mile."

"Then let me strap you on my back as the porter Indians in the Andes carry people."

"No, no, monsieur; you have done quite enough," said Hortense. "Wait until morning."

"But suppose De Gourges and all his fleet should be gone?"

"God will provide for me, monsieur. Whatever may happen, I will trust wholly in Him."

He made her a bed of leaves and branches, spread a soft Indian tanned robe upon it, and Hortense slept sweetly, while he sat all night long by the watch-fire in silence.

Next morning he awoke the sleepy Indians at daylight, and, after an early breakfast, the party set out for the river in which the French fleet was anchored.

Francisco Estevan's own future was dark and uncertain. Hortense knew he was not going to France, and though she was anxious to know what he would do, she refrained from asking him. Having been pardoned by Melendez, and being a Spaniard, Francisco had decided in his own

mind to go to St. Augustine and await an opportunity to return to Cuba. He had been away
from his home so many years, and such a great
length of time had elapsed since relatives and
friends had heard from him, that they no doubt
long since had given him up for dead. His return
at this late day would be like a resurrection from
the tomb.

With these thoughts he was beguiling the tedium
of the morning march, when one of the Indians
carrying the litter informed him that on reaching
the top of a hill a short distance before them they
would be able to see the river.

"Travel faster," urged the impatient Spaniard.
"Travel faster, for we have no time to lose. We
must reach the river before the French ships sail."

"We go as fast as we can," answered one of the
carriers.

The consuming anxiety of the moment caused the
perspiration to start on Estevan's face. He ran
ahead of the carriers, and, gaining the summit from
which he had a view of the harbor and ocean,
saw the white sails of the French fleet far out to
sea.

"Too late—too late!" he groaned, leaning
against a tree.

The Indians came up and placed the litter on the
ground. Hortense gazed off over the bay and the
19

sea at the sails of those homeward-bound ships.
She did not weep; she did not sigh; but, patient
and resigned to the last, she gazed calmly after the
departing vessels.   By her side stood Francisco,
more overcome than she.   He grasped her hand,
their eyes met, and for a moment they gazed in
silence at each other.

The great moment in Francisco's life had come,
and it was like other moments.   His doom was
spoken in a word.   A single look from the eyes,
a single pressure from the hand decided it before
the lips could speak.   For a moment his agitation
was perceptible, even to the savages; then a change
came over his face.   He grew calmer, and, turning
to the carriers, signed them to go away.   They
understood that he wished to be alone with the lily
and left them.   Turning to her, he said in a voice
strangely calm, yet which seemed to come from
the depths of his soul:

"Hortense, God has decreed it."

She turned her inquiring eyes on him, and after
waiting a moment to gain control over his emotions,
he pointed to the French sails just disappearing
over the horizon and repeated:

"God has decreed it; why longer try to resist
the will of Heaven?"

His manner and his words were an enigma to
her, and she answered:

"Monsieur, you speak strangely. I—I do not understand you."

"Listen to me, Hortense. The scales have fallen from my eyes, and I see the hand of God in it all from the beginning."

Her blue eyes grew round with wonder, and she was almost ready to doubt his sanity. Why did his face glow with joy and rapture? Why did he cling to her hand while his breath came rapidly, as if he labored under some great excitement? Before she could speak he added:

"Yes, Hortense, from the beginning to the present hour I clearly see the hand of God which decrees that which must be. Go back to the hour of our first meeting. Why was I the only one saved from the wreck? Why should I be rescued, and by you, if God had not some design? I tore myself rudely away from you and lived a miserable existence until again we met. When we were attacked by the pirate ship, I, of all the passengers and crew, was spared. When the French bore away to Fort Carolinia, I alone of all was brought here. Why should it be so, if God had not wished it?"

She watched him, her great earnest eyes filled with wonder, while her heart beat wildly. He went on:

"If God did not decree it, why were you brought

where I was? I did not expect it, neither did you. The meeting was not planned by us, but by God. Why was I able to rescue you from among so many others and place you with Saturiova, if God had not designed it? It was God who designed that you should in turn rescue me, and that we should be left to each other in this strange New World. O Hortense! are you still as blind as I have been? Do you not know that we were designed for each other?"

She was dumb with amazement, her heart palpitating, her face radiant with hope and joy, her breath coming by quick gasps, while her breast heaved tumultuously. In his earnestness he had knelt beside the litter and clasped her small hand in both his own, while his dark, piercing eyes, filled with melting tenderness, looked into hers.

"Hortense, God planned it; God wills it; let us not resist His wish. Be my own—my wife, Hortense."

It was some moments before she could speak; then she said in a faint voice:

"Your monastic vows?"

"I have altered my course in life and I will not become a priest. Our religions differ; but if, as you once said, all the church of God will in the end be one grand brotherhood, let us be first to unite the two faiths. Promise to become my wife,

"GOD WILLS IT; BE MY WIFE, HORTENSE."

Hortense, and I swear by all the saints on the calendar and by the great God whom we worship that
I will make you a true and faithful husband."

She essayed to speak, but language failed.
This was the realization of her dearest dream, for
which she had never dared hope. Putting her
arms about his neck, she whispered:

" Yes, God wills it."

He rose like one whose plans in life are all made,
and stood by the side of the girl whose protection
and support he was henceforth to be.

Before either had time to speak, they saw a tall
young Indian approaching. It was the gallant
Olacatora. He was hunting for them, and, as their
attendants had failed to return, Francisco asked
him to aid in carrying Hortense to the house of
Saturiova, to which Olacatora assented.

They passed along a solitary forest road, cool
and dark in the shadow of the woods, but hot and
glaring where it emerged and dipped into the
valley. In the valley was a pretty Indian village
of the picturesque aboriginese pattern stretched
along the banks of the river, which wound through
green savannahs and orange-groves. In the out-
skirts of the village was a picturesque lodge, the
home of the chief, Saturiova.

A forest maiden of nineteen or twenty years of
age was coming along the road alone. She was an

olive-checked damsel, with the fine, delicate beauty
of the wild flower, so rare among the natives of
America.   Her costume, wild and becoming, of
the finest fawn-skin, ornamented with furs and
bright feathers, added to her beauty and grace.

Her wealth of luxuriant
hair fell about her inno-
cent face and down upon
the shapely shoulders.
One hand held a bou-
quet of wild flowers,
and the other hung list-
lessly at her side.   Her eyes
were bright, as if expecting some
"A Forest Maiden." one from the forest, and her
breath came quick, while her cherry lips, parted
by the smile of an angel, revealed two rows of
pearls.   She suddenly discovered a strange group
approaching the village.   Two men were carrying
a litter on which sat a maiden of the same age as
the one just described, though fair as the morning.

The smile brightened, a cry of joy escaped the
lips of the daughter of Saturiova; she ran to the
litter, and the maid of the morning and the maiden
of twilight were clasped in each other's arms, each
murmuring in endearing tones:

" My sister!"

The wanderer had returned.   Old Saturiova was

found sitting in front of his lodge smoking his pipe, and he evinced no more surprise or concern at the return of Francisco Estevan than if he had been gone but a day instead of two years.

Hortense was taken to her lodge, where her red sister ministered to her wants. She gathered from the forest leaves and roots known to possess medicinal properties, beat them into poultices, and bandaged the poor little wounded feet.

Francisco Estevan was invited to dine with the chief, after which he had a long talk with the Indian, in which he expressed his sincerest thanks for the tender care with which Saturiova had protected and guarded Hortense.

"She is my own daughter," said Saturiova, "and I would have defended her with my life."

"You did well."

"Must I give her up?"

The question somewhat startled Francisco, inasmuch as it suggested the possibility of a new danger. Should he inform the Indian of his intention to take her away, he feared the savage might conceal her in such a way that he would not find her. After a moment he answered:

"She will always be the daughter of the great chief who so nobly protected her, for she has no other father on earth. She may go to live in another lodge some day, as will your red daughter when she marries; but both will ever love their good father Saturiova."

The chief answered by a grunt of satisfaction, and from that moment Estevan knew he had won the chief, and Hortense would be safe in his keeping. He lingered a few days at the Indian village, while Hortense rapidly recovered under the treatment of her red sister. On the third day after her arrival she was able to walk about.

It was again evening. The soft southern moon, round and full, rose in the heavens, shedding a flood of silver light over the orange-groves and tropical everglades, which have long been a synonym for grandeur and beauty. The air was burdened with perfume and all the sounds peculiar to the tropics.

Francisco and Hortense wandered to a seat beneath a large tree and sat for a long time listening to the sounds of nature. At last she spoke:

"When do you go?"

"In the morning."

"To St. Augustine?"

"Yes."

"Are you quite sure you can safely return?"

"Why not?" he answered. "I have been pardoned for all past offences and have committed none since."

"No,"

Another silence of several moments' duration followed, and she asked:

"Will you be long gone?"

"No. I cannot say how long; but it will be until I am able to return and take you home with me. There you shall become mine, and when you are my wife I can defend you against all powers, Christian or pagan."

"Even against Mendoza?"

"Mendoza is my friend."

"And Melendez?"

"Melendez will not dare act contrary to the wishes of his chaplain."

For a few moments they sat gazing at the far-off southern moon and the soft bright-eyed stars which seemed to sparkle and wink in approval. He was the first to break the silence.

"Hortense, ours has been a stormy life. It has been a long, hard road we have travelled; but there is happiness at the end. God has led us by many steep and thorny paths, over many a stormy sea; but He has brought us to rest and happiness."

She clung fondly to him and murmured:

"Francisco, the joy of this moment seems to repay me for the terrible past. God is good."

"Let us hope that this is the dawn of a brighter existence which will not end with this life, but will continue throughout eternity."

They talked of the future as only betrothed
couples do. That future was bright to them, although of this world's goods they had nothing save
each other; but what more did they want? They
were in a new world.

The stars never shone so brightly before, the
moon never seemed to flood the earth with such
mellow light; the murmur of the cascade was never
so gentle; the carols of the night birds never so
musical. All nature was in harmony with those
who were in harmony with God. It is only when
we become rebellious against nature and nature's
God that we fail to see the glorious beauties which
lie in abundance about us.

Next morning Estevan was to set out for St.
Augustine to beard the lion in his den and ask
only life and peace in the New World. The parting
was short and affecting. Hortense accompanied
him a short distance; then he bade her adieu,
clasped her a moment to his breast, imprinted a
kiss on her cheek and was gone, while she returned to her lodge to shed a few tears and pray
that his efforts might be crowned with success.

There arose from behind a cluster of flowering
shrubs a tall, dark man, his great, burning eyes
for a moment fixed on the lodge in which Hortense
had disappeared, and then turned toward Estevan's
retreating form, but dimly visible far down the

road. His face was grave, and for a long time he stood motionless as a statue. What a whirlwind of tempestuous emotions, what a conflict between right and wrong was raging in the breast of that savage! Yet the most astute reader of physiognomy could not have determined from the fixed and immovable face that his soul was not as calm as a summer sea.

Olacatora was fighting a battle which has to be fought by more than half of Mother Eve's sons—a conflict requiring more heroism than he displayed when, ˙alone and single-handed, he charged the gunner of Fort St. Mattheo. Jealous passion and reason were arrayed against each other, and at times, when his hand convulsively clutched his weapon, it seemed as if hate would conquer. Reason and gentleness in the end prevailed, however, and, with his face as mild as the holy morn, he gazed long at the lodge and murmured:

"It is better. He is of her race and I am only her red brother."

Then he turned slowly about and plunged into the forest in an opposite direction to that taken by Francisco Estevan.

CHAPTER XX.

TIME sped swiftly on. St. Augustine lay on the shore of the river where her great fort and bristling guns seemed defying the armies and navies of the world. It was about six o'clock in the evening. The heat of the day had gradually decreased and a light evening breeze arose, seeming like the respiration of nature on awaking from a burning siesta of the south. A small Spanish sloop, chaste and elegant in form, was gliding into the peaceful harbor. The motion resembled that of a swan with its wings opened toward the wind. By the skilful manœuvring of the man at the helm it swept gracefully into the bay, leaving behind a glittering track. By degrees the sun disappeared behind its western horizon; but, as though to prove the truth of the fanciful ideas in heathen mythology, its indiscreet rays reappeared on the summit of each wave, seeming to show that the god of fire had enfolded himself in the bosom of Amphitrite, who in vain endeavored to hide her lover beneath her azure mantle. The little vessel moved rapidly on, though there did not seem to be sufficient wind to ruffle the curls on the head of a young girl. Standing in the bow was a tall man of dark complexion, whose dress and air indicated the Spanish sailor of the period. He observed with dilating eyes that they were approaching the dark mass, bristling with cannon, known as the Fort of St. Augustine.

Sitting in the stern of the little vessel thus gliding toward the Spanish fort were Francisco Estevan and Hortense De Barre, peaceful and smiling as the skies above them and the gentle sea about them. All the storm clouds seemed to have rolled away from their horizon, and the sorrows of the past were but a dark background on which was to be painted the golden happiness of the future. Their marriage made in heaven, despite the bigotry of the age which had so long kept two loving hearts apart, was soon to be celebrated on earth. They had grown like two trees, whose roots and branches are intertwined and whose perfume rises together to the skies.

Francisco Estevan on his arrival at St. Augustine, after leaving Hortense as related in the last chapter, had found Melendez quite changed. He received with kindness his countryman whom he had so greatly wronged. The terrible lesson of De Gourges had humbled the pride of the haughty bigot, who knew that his harsh and inhuman conduct toward the Huguenots had been severely criticised by the best nations of Europe, for the age of bigotry was on the wane. Though he justified himself for the atrocious act by the remembrance that the men, women, and children whom he had ruthlessly swept out of existence were heretics, and that he acted under the orders of his king, he could but feel that the retribution visited upon him by the French was to have been expected.

He was in an humble, almost penitent mood when Mendoza came to him with Francisco Estevan, who had just come in from the forest, whither, it was represented, he had fled at the approach of the French. In the great whirlpool of exciting events which had followed the attack on the forts, Melendez had almost, if not quite, forgotten Francisco Estevan. As he had not appeared after his release, it was generally thought that he had perished in the attack, and Mendoza had offered up many prayers for his soul. The Spanish admiral was pleased to find him alive and congratulated him on his escape.

Francisco told briefly the story of his wrongs and the deceptions practised by John Gyrot, who had met his fate at his own hands in the forest.

Melendez listened calmly, with but little show of emotion, and when he had finished said:

"It is but human to err, and often we may find in this transitory life a demon in the deceitful guise of a man. It was so in this case."

Before going to Melendez, Francisco had made a full and complete confession to Mendoza of his love for Hortense De Barre, and expressed his wish that she be allowed to come to the Spanish settlement to be made his wife according to the ceremonies and rules of the Catholic Church. Though living in that age of bigotry, Mendoza was a person who could accommodate his conscience and religion to suit the circumstances and wishes of his friends; and though general custom, if not church law, forbade the marriage of a Catholic to a Protestant, he gave the match his approval, and was quite sure that, after so many wonderful events combining to bring about the happy union of Francisco and Hortense, it must be the will of God. There is no doubt that Mendoza hoped to proselyte the fair Huguenot when once she was the wife of such a firm Catholic as Francisco Estevan. It was Mendoza who made the plea for the French maiden to the Spanish admiral and asked that she who had been an object of Gyrot's persecution from childhood be permitted to come to St. Augustine to dwell.

After listening to his spiritual adviser, Melendez, in giving his consent, among other things said:

"She was a heretic, and doubtless is yet. If it is our duty to convert the heathen to the true religion, may we not hope also to proselyte a heretic, to induce her to return to the true faith which she has abandoned? Let her come; let the young man make her his wife. We will be doing nothing inconsistent with the spirit and genius of our institutions. We should do nothing for revenge, though everything for security; nothing for the past, but everything for the present and future."

Next day Estevan attended mass and spent a long time in solemn conversation with the priest over the future The young Spaniard was happy, and that evening he set out in the sloop which was described as returning at the beginning of this chapter. He sailed along the coast to the mouth of the river near the banks of which was the home of Saturiova. Leaving his sloop at anchor in charge of the small crew which had accompanied him, he proceeded on foot and alone to the Indian village, where Hortense waited to greet him. The day after his arrival, accompanied by the chief and his family, Francisco and Hortense set out for the sloop which was to convey them to St. Augustine. They tried in vain to prevail on Saturiova and his daughter to accompany them. The old chief dared not risk himself in the hands of the Spaniards after all that had occurred, so after an affectionate farewell the lovers went aboard the little vessel and sailed out of the harbor toward St. Augustine.

The sombre shades of twilight had begun to gather, the moon hung over the western forest, and the pale glow of an evening star shot athwart the path of the dying day, as the sloop glided into the harbor of St. Augustine. Suddenly there came from the fort a blinding flash and the boom of a cannon, and then three more in quick succession. The four sailors on the sloop stood in the bow with the pans of their guns open and match-cords lighted, and when the cannon fired they answered the salute. A cheer went up from the shore, which was thronged with people; for the romantic story of Francisco and Hortense had been noised abroad, and the entire village turned out to meet the lovers.

Hortense, clothed in the garb of civilization, stepped ashore and was greeted with another cheer. Among the throng were many of the Huguenot women and children who had been spared from the massacre at Carolinia. Everybody seemed to rejoice in the happy termination of the adventures of the lovers, and all praised God that the age of bigotry was past, giving way to the dawn of reason.

20

A Huguenot widow who had lost her husband
in the massacre at Carolinia, and who had since
lived with the conquerors, took Hortense to her
home until her marriage, which was to be celebrated
as soon as her husband, with the aid of his friends,
could erect a suitable house to live in.

Francisco had given up all thought of returning
to Cuba.   His parents had no doubt mourned him
as dead, even if they were themselves in the land
of the living.   Now that he had decided to rebel
against their cherished wishes and was to marry
a Huguenot, he could not shock their religious
sense with the knowledge.   His wife, a Protestant, would never be received as a daughter by his
Catholic mother, so he resolved to remain dead to
his parents.   In this New World he would begin
a new career, and carve out for himself a name
for liberality, reason, and humanity which would
glow like a beacon light in the coming age.

The Spaniards gave him their aid in building
his house.   It was only a log hut, built after the
primitive fashion, but was very neat and tidy, the
walls hewn straight and whitewashed inside.   All
worked with a will, for the good people were elated
at the thought that their colony was to soon witness the first Christian marriage ever celebrated
in Florida, fifty-six years after its discovery.   A
man whose grandfather came with Columbus on

his first voyage of discovery to the New World was to wed a beauty from France. No wonder the colony was thrown into a flutter of excitement.

Good Spanish dames joined the good French women in arranging for the event, and the fair bride-elect found herself overwhelmed with kindness. What a glorious dawn after such an awful night!

The day for the wedding festivities came at last, and the Spanish colony put on a holiday appearance. The little church was decorated within and without with gay wild flowers. Every official was present, even Melendez, who had volunteered to give away the bride. The little chapel was adorned and decorated until it looked like a bit of fairyland.

At last, when all things were in readiness, the people sang a solemn chant, at the close of which the bride and groom entered the chapel. Hortense was dressed in a beautiful Spanish robe, very fashionable at that day, with a neat, modest ruff, and her arms, bare to the shoulders, sparkled with jewels, the presents of her warm-hearted, sympathetic friends. Her bridal veil was such as one would hardly expect to see in this new land. It was of the finest gauze, like a fleecy cloud from the skilful looms of old Cadiz, and it adorned the most lovely being in all Florida.

Francisco Estevan was attired in the gay costume of a Spanish cavalier of the period, wearing the sword of a gentleman at his side. He was a noble specimen of manly beauty—a splendid form, with the carriage of one born to command, and she was the ideal of womanly modesty, loveliness, and simplicity.

By the altar, in sacerdotal robes, stood the priest to officiate at this sacred, joyous, and most interesting of all ceremonies. After the usual prayers and *Te Deums*, in a solemn and impressive manner, he pronounced the marriage according to the Roman Catholic Church, and thus wed the Catholic and Huguenot before the grass grew green on the graves of those slain through avarice, hate, and religious bigotry.

Francisco and Hortense went at once to their humble home, where they began life together with a fair promise of happiness and tranquillity.

The Spaniards were left by the evacuation of De Gourges for many years without competitors in Florida, and they applied themselves to fortifying and improving their settlement at St. Augustine. Fort St. Mattheo was suffered for a while to go to decay, and then was rebuilt under the name of San Juan, or St. John, the name given the river. St. Augustine continued to grow and flourish, and though it has never become a great commercial city, it enjoys the distinction of being the first and oldest town in the United States of America. Francisco Estevan and his wife became permanent citizens of St. Augustine, and they and their descendants figured prominently in the many stirring events from which was evolved the greatest nation on earth.

THE END.

HISTORICAL INDEX.

CHRONOLOGY.

PERIOD III.—AGE OF BIGOTRY.

A.D. 1547 TO A.D. 1570.

1529. REFORMATION BY MARTIN LUTHER commenced.

1547. ACCESSION OF EDWARD VI. to throne of France, —Jan. 28.

1553. ACCESSION OF MARY I. to throne of England, —July 6.

PERSECUTION OF ENGLISH PURITANS commenced.

1558. ACCESSION OF ELIZABETH to throne of England,— Nov. 17.

1561. COLIGNI secured a patent from Charles IX. to settle Huguenots in Florida.

1562. RIBAULT sailed from Dieppe, France, with two vessels of Huguenots, to settle in Florida,— Feb. 18.

1563. HUGUENOTS left by Ribault in Florida abandon the country.

1564. LAUDONNIÈRE with Huguenots sailed from Havre de Grace for Florida,—April 23.

HUGUENOTS settled in Florida and built Fort Carolina on St. John's River.

JOHN CALVIN died in Switzerland.

1565. RIBAULT joined Laudonnière at Fort Carolina.

MELENDEZ FOUNDED ST. AUGUSTINE, oldest European town in the United States,—Aug. 29.

MELENDEZ massacred Huguenots on St. John's River.

1567. DE GOURGES sailed with men and vessels to avenge the Huguenots,—Aug. 22.

1568. DE GOURGES MASSACRED THE SPANISH and hanged some on the spot of Melendez' massacre in retribution.

THE

COLUMBIAN HISTORICAL NOVELS

A COMPLETE HISTORY OF OUR COUNTRY,

FROM THE TIME OF COLUMBUS DOWN TO THE PRESENT DAY, IN THE FORM
OF TWELVE COMPLETE STORIES.

BY

JOHN R. MUSICK.

ONE HUNDRED HALF-TONE PLATES, MAPS OF THE PERIOD, AND NUMEROUS
PEN-AND-INK DRAWINGS, BY F. A. CARTER.

TITLES:

NEW YORK

FUNK & WAGNALLS COMPANY

LONDON AND TORONTO

1895

www.ingramcontent.com/pod-product-compliance
Lightning Source LLC
Chambersburg PA
CBHW021801110726

47902CB00006B/1603